The Stars We Walked Upon

By

M.L. Bullock

This book is dedicated to all the fans of the *Seven Sisters* series. Thank you for walking through the Blue Room and strolling down the shady paths of the Moonlight Garden with me.

May you have many dreams, and may they all come true.

O Stars and Dreams and Gentle Night;
O Night and Stars return!
And hide me from the hostile light
That does not warm, but burn

That drains the blood of suffering men;
Drinks tears, instead of dew:
Let me sleep through his blinding reign,
And only wake with you!

—Emily Bronte

Excerpt from "Stars"

Prologue

Mobile, AL, 1851

Sunlight splashed through the tall conservatory windows, and I leaned back in the comfortable parlor chair, a glass of brandy in my hand. I closed my eyes, allowing the music to carry me to places far and away. The sound of the piano lent to the illusion of sanity and comfort, two things perpetually absent from my world of escalating darkness. The notes were light and choppy and full of happiness. If I allowed myself to, I could imagine I was in the music room of some talented debutante hoping to impress me, the elegant Captain David Garrett.

How many times had this been the case? How many musical recitals had been performed for me?

Sipping my brandy, I scanned through the memories with pleasure. The first face I recalled was that of the delightful Katrina Phelps, the daughter of Christian and Mary Beth Phelps of Savannah, Georgia. A pretty thing with light brown eyes, a sharp, clever wit and a sultry voice, a voice too sultry for one so young. Still, as charming as her face and figure were, she had not yielded to my ardent desire despite my best efforts to persuade her. The Phelps family welcomed me into their particular society; that is until that wretched letter arrived. And then Katrina was lost to me.

Ah, but there was always a fly in the ointment. One sour spinster who could not or would not leave the past alone. Yes, the past was my constant companion. I shook the memory of Miss Phelps and her tearstained face away. How she cried over me! At the time, I believed that I loved her—imagine that!

Oh yes, then there was Miss Virginia Lewis. The mother was so keen to make my acquaintance that I barely knew whom to seduce—the mother or the daughter. However, after meeting the woman's husband, I decided that the latter would suffice. Unlike many of the maidens I dabbled with, I had not been able to control myself, so willing was she. I did partake of the young woman's delights and so perhaps deserved the disdain of Red Hills' society, but in the end, what did I care? Red Hills was no Savannah, nor Charleston nor even a Mobile. It was merely a farm community, and Miss Virginia Lewis nothing more than a glamorous wealthy farm girl with hefty arms, pink cheeks and skin that tasted like butter. My cheeks warmed at the thought of her, or perhaps it was the brandy. I smiled remembering our times together in the milk shed, the store cupboard, the floor of the carriage. But I had been a much younger man then, just hitting my prime.

The piano's notes climbed higher and the music became lighter. I yielded myself to the tune, pausing only to sip the decadent drink in my crystal glass. I felt as if the notes could almost carry me to heaven—it was probably as close to that holy place as I could ever hope to reach.

Especially after what happened to Miss Cottonwood. Dear, sweet, gentle Miss Cottonwood. Now she had been a true lady. *That had not been entirely my fault.* The girl must have been out of her mind to seek me aboard the Delta Queen—or been encouraged to do so by someone other than me. With slitted eyes I observed my nude piano player. Loose coils of long blond hair hung down her back and stuck to her skin. How she sweated when we made love! She was no pasty-faced farm girl happy to endure whatever pleased me. No, she was an active participant—curious, hungry and eager to please and be pleased. It occurred to me that I should love her. After all, we were bound together in a dark world of our own making; perhaps I did love her in my own perverse way.

Although I told myself that she was the bane of my existence I admired her ambition, her skilled depravities. How I loved her constant scheming—her spirited aspirations far exceeded mine. She was like that biblical hussy Jezebel, and she deserved to be thrown out of the tower. I was the doomed Ahab.

I knew all this, and yet I was her slave.

Suddenly the piano made a crashing noise as her hands slammed down on the keys. Quick as a flash she was off her tufted stool and standing before me. Her damp tresses covered her goblet-shaped breasts.

"What are you thinking? I demand you tell me!"

As subtly as I could, I glanced at her hands to make sure that they held no object that might injure me, for my love had a deadly temper. Seeing no scissors, knitting needles or any other type of blade, I smiled at her peacefully.

"I think of nothing but you, my love. What else should I think of?"

"You're a fool! Tell me you're not thinking of her!" Her hands went to the curve of her naked hips, and she stared at me with unbelieving eyes.

"Calm down, dearest. Sit in my lap. Let us talk of the future—not the past. You promised, remember?"

I could see the struggle in her eyes as she gave in to my request and smiled that catlike smile. Her arms snaked about my neck, and her frame was as light as a feather as she perched in my lap. With insincere calmness I stroked her hair as she plunged her hand in my open shirt and rubbed my chest lightly. "Now. Where shall we go next, darling?" I spoke carefully in soothing tones. "To Paris? Perhaps to Boston? Where shall I take you?" She kissed my neck with her childlike lips—lips that always tasted of lemonade. How she loved the drink! "Nectar of the gods," she called it as she added ridiculous amounts of gin into her glass.

"I want to see *all* of those places, my darling captain. All of them! But we must wait a little while."

I wondered what plan she had concocted in her feverish brain. Isla Beaumont rarely kept me in mind when she planned a scheme. Why should today be any different? She took my hand with her small one and kissed it. "Good news, my love. I am with child."

I was shocked into silence. I weighed her mood to determine how to proceed.

"Isn't that delightful?"

I responded with a confident smile. "If you are happy, I am happy. I must say I have never considered myself a family man. My, how you have changed me."

She giggled. "Oh no, darling. I am quite sure that I am carrying a Cottonwood. A long-awaited boy for Jeremiah Cottonwood. Won't he be delighted to hear the news that he will finally have a son!" She hopped out of my lap and spun about as if she were in the ballroom.

It was my turn to laugh. The whole thing seemed so outlandish I could not wrap my mind around it. "You and Cottonwood? Tell me, my clever love. How did you ever manage that? It was my understanding that the man had no appreciation for young beauties such as yourself, not of the female persuasion."

She curtsied graciously, lifting the edges of a pretend dress. "Never underestimate my skills. That would be a mistake. He was like clay in my hands." She giggled again and pretended to hide a nonexistent blush.

I raised my glass to her and said, "Well done."

She frowned. "You do not seem as pleased as I imagined you would be. Isn't this the cleverest thing? Just think. In a few months we will have what we wanted—Seven Sisters! Oh, and that is just the beginning! Imagine me with a fat little baby and all that money. Won't that be funny?"

"Not to doubt your amazing ability to make men do whatever you desire, but what makes you believe that Mr. Cottonwood will welcome this news? We all know that man is an evil-tempered drunk."

"I have it all planned out."

"I had no doubt of that."

"You must trust me, dear Captain. I will tell you more later, but now I need a distraction—a 'faveur discrète'. Let us go upstairs and celebrate!"

I swirled the rest of my brandy and tossed it down my throat. The warmth of it invigorated me. Now wasn't the time to consider the meaning of all this. I would do that when she slept—whenever she slept. Sometimes she would not sleep for days. I pulled her close to me and stared down into her cherub-like face. How could such a face hide such a mind?

"You are full of surprises, my sweet one."

"Happy surprises?" Her coy look stirred my loins.

"Are there any other kind?" I scooped her up in my arms. She kissed my neck as I stepped over the body of our hostess. I accidentally kicked her and foolishly offered an "Excuse me."

To that, she giggled again. "David," she whispered in my ear, "Lennie Ree can't hear you. She's dead."

By the time we made it upstairs, I was nearly naked and completely hers.

***

Hours later I slipped out of our stolen bed to go downstairs in search of food. I was thinking not only for myself but also for my beloved, who was always ravenous after a murder. Now that she was with child, I was sure she would be even hungrier. But I needed food myself too. This was no small house—surely there would be something hidden in a larder somewhere. Maybe even some lemonade for my Isla.

Being the lover of the demanding, demented cherub took a lot of energy, and I needed to build my strength. I walked down the stairs holding up my trousers with one hand and whistling. I paused at the bottom step to give a respectful nod to our dead hostess. Just as I stepped over her the front door opened—there was nowhere to hide. The housekeeper, a tall, thin woman dressed in all black, did not see me at first. She set her basket down on the entryway table and left her purse there while she removed her plain black hat. I could see by her demeanor she was not someone to be trifled with—a no-nonsense kind of woman.

I decided to take the bull by the horns. Some women preferred to be charmed into doing whatever it was I wanted them to do; others preferred the direct approach. I chose the second option and hoped for the right results. If she failed to amuse me, then of course we would simply have to kill her too.

"And who might you be?" I asked in a commanding voice.

The woman appeared calm, not shocked in the least by what she saw or by my question. She had not run out the door, which she very well could have. Out of respect, I buttoned my trousers and my open shirt.

"Docie Loxley is my name. I am the housekeeper."

"Well, Miss Loxley, it appears that my hostess has had an accident and died."

"That much I see, and it is a shame. I have not been paid in six months. Who's going to give me my wages now?" She walked toward the stiff body of Lennie Ree Meadows and touched her with the toe of her black boot as if she wanted to make sure she was dead. She needn't have bothered.

Isla said from behind me, "We should bury her. But somewhere where dogs won't find her. You don't want the dead to come back. They smell awful." She hopped on my back as if she were a child and I a child's party entertainer. I did not argue but gave her a piggyback ride up and down the stairs. Isla giggled with pleasure. At least she was clothed now, although her hair was mussed and she smelled of our lovemaking. She slid off my back and stepped gingerly over our hostess. She presented herself to the housekeeper, her hands on her hips. If the housekeeper knew that her life was in the young woman's hands, if she understood that Isla could and would kill her if it pleased her, she gave no sign. She sighed and said to her, "You needn't bother yourself with this mess. I will bury her after breakfast. She's not in any hurry. Are you hungry?"

Apparently deciding the housekeeper should live, Isla bobbed alongside, free spirit that she was, and followed her into the larder. I heard Isla ask her as if it were the most natural thing, "After you bury the old lady, would you mind helping me get my hair in order? It's a rat's nest."

I didn't hear the woman's reply but if she had given the wrong one, I would have heard Isla's angry scream. As they left, I stole a tablecloth from a nearby table and covered the deceased woman's body. "Again, my apologies, madam." Leaving her in Miss Loxley's hands, I walked away from the whole mess in search of more brandy.

Now there were three of us—three savages and all with black hearts.

Chapter One—Carrie Jo

"Dang it!" I woke myself up again faced with a choice—either put my size-seven foot on Ashland's behind and kick him off our brand new canopy bed or get up and leave. After five nights of unintentional access into his less than faithful dreams I had had about enough. It was too late to get into a knock-down, drag-out fight, so I decided to take the high road. In an angry huff, I sat up like a snapped rubber band and threw back the covers. Naturally, he didn't flinch.

Of course not! Why should he stop dreaming about some curvaceous supermodel while I'm fuming right beside him?

I stared down at the perfectly peaceful face of my sleeping husband, and my heart was a ball of feelings—none of them good. I couldn't decide which I hated more: that I couldn't control my dream catching or that I couldn't stop thinking about what I saw. Maybe it was just that I wouldn't be able to sleep for the rest of the night—God, I was tired! Call me sensitive, but the images of wanton women twisting under my husband in the throes of passion were just a bit more than I could bear. The last thing I wanted to do was fall asleep again and "enjoy" the big finish.

He's lucky we have a housekeeper who likes to cook for him because I sure as hell won't be making him breakfast! Not this morning!

Still, in the back of my mind I knew how this would play out. He'd wake up as chipper as a beaver with a new log without a clue as to why I was so pissed. I sure couldn't come out and tell him. Nope. No way was I giving up the high ground now. I might have issues, but I wasn't the cheater. I'd slap a big ol' fake Carrie Jo smile on my face and pretend that everything was right as rain. Thankfully, he did not have women's intuition. For someone who had extrasensory gifts, Ashland Stuart was none too perceptive—at least not when it came to me.

Swearing under my breath, I got out of bed and walked to the large round window across the room. The moon glowed round and near-perfect above the city of Mobile. A few wisps of clouds passed in front of it, but they quickly skittered away as the breeze blew in and along with it the fog from the nearby bay. According to the weatherman, the temperatures were never this warm in January, but people didn't seem to mind. They liked wearing flip-flops and T-shirts even in the dead of winter. As my old friend Bette used to tell me, "If you don't like the weather in Mobile, just wait a few minutes, dah-ling. It will change!" She'd chuckle and shake her head in amusement, white curls bouncing with every shake. I wondered what advice she'd have for me now. She loved Ashland, that much I knew. I had known her less than a year and she was thirty years my senior, but she had truly become one of my best friends ever. I missed her every single day. She had been a second mom—a confidante, my protector. I loved her.

I leaned against the window with arms crossed and stared down at the quiet downtown streets below. From the top floor of our Victorian home, the view was peaceful, with the exception of the occasional siren from the nearby police station. My friend and assistant Rachel informed me that the quiet façade would quickly fade when Mardi Gras kicked off in a few weeks. Apparently it was such a parking and traffic nightmare that she'd already developed maps to help us navigate traffic and avoid the bead-hungry, moon-pie-seeking masses. We even changed our office hours to accommodate the local parade calendar. I looked over my shoulder at Ashland—he didn't stir. Typical.

Think about something else, Carrie Jo!

I tried to distract myself with thoughts of work. I still couldn't believe I had an office—a real business of my own. Word had gotten out about my role in the restoration of Seven Sisters and the additions to the facility. Those old plantation owners were beginning to see what a lucrative venture restoring these beautiful downtown homes truly was. Of course I could not take all the credit. It took a team, and many of those team members were no longer with us. Like it did so often recently, my mind traveled back to the first time I visited this charming yet dangerous city. Some people called Mobile the Azalea City; others called it the Port City. In my own experience I believed a better name would be the Supernatural City. I had never been to New Orleans, but I was pretty sure that old city had nothing on this one.

I nervously spun the white gold wedding band on my finger and stared at the shiny ring in the moonlight. Tears flooded my eyes. We'd fought so hard to keep it all together, and now here I was staring out the window unable to sleep beside the man I loved. I did love him, and he loved me. I would just have to figure out a way to get my dream catching under control.

Suddenly I felt two hands on my shoulders. I gasped and nearly jumped out of my skin. I turned to find a laughing Ashland standing behind me with his hands raised in surrender. "Sorry! I thought you heard me. I didn't mean to startle you."

"What the hell?"

He laughed again. Normally I would find the sound cheerful, even sexy. Now I just wanted to slap him. He said in a softer voice, "You were deep in thought. I didn't mean to scare you like that."

"Well, you did. Let me catch my breath."

"I've got a better idea. Why don't you come back to bed? Maybe I can find a way to soothe your nerves?" He rubbed my shoulder, but I didn't encourage him.

I stammered for a moment, then stomped to the bed and grabbed my blanket, intending to find sleep elsewhere. "I can't sleep. You go to bed. No sense in both of us being tired." Playfully he grabbed the other end. He still had no clue how mad I really was. He had no idea that I knew about his breast-centric dreams. "Let go, Ashland!"

"What did I do? I said I was sorry. Now come to bed."

I glared at him. Unless I was willing to tell him the truth, I would have to do as he asked. "Fine! I just hope I can sleep. My eyes are going to look horrible in the morning, and I have to meet with Desmond Taylor. You know, you've had me up every night this week."

"What? Have I been snoring? I'm sorry, Carrie Jo. Maybe I should get some of those strips for my nose—the kind that keeps your airways open. You should have said something sooner." I flopped in the bed and turned my back to him, beating my pillow into submission. He tucked the blanket around me and kissed me on the cheek.

Darn him! How dare he be kind! I like being mad at him.

"I promise to pick some up tomorrow, and don't worry about Taylor. You're a genius. He would be lucky to have you work on his project. In the meantime, if my snoring gets really bad I can go sleep in the guest room. Should I?"

I sighed, guilt over my snooping washing over me. "That won't be necessary." As he put his arm around me and held me, I realized I was being a fool. A man's mind was his own territory—it belonged solely to him, and that included his dreams. How would I like it if Ashland saw a few of my dreams? I never planned to dream some of the crazy stuff I did, but it happened. I let him cuddle up to me, and I enjoyed his clean sandalwood scent and his strong arms. *Well, as long as he's only dreaming about it and not acting upon it, then we should be okay. Chances are he doesn't even remember them. Most people don't remember their dreams at all.* Still, I had to do something if I wanted to stay married. And indeed I did.

I glanced back at the clock on the bedside table. It was 4:45. Weird. What were the odds of that happening again? I had woken myself up early every day since Monday. Now it was Friday night—no, make that

Saturday morning. As I pondered the puzzle, my eyes grew heavy and I soon fell back to sleep.

I chose to think about something else for a while. Like Delilah Iverson. I'd put her to the side too long. I had promised myself after my friends died (they did die, didn't they?) that I would dig in deeper. If for no other reason than to honor their lives. I hadn't kept my word, which wasn't like me at all.

Conjuring her image from my memory of our ballroom encounter, I whispered her name. It felt right to seek the ghosts of the past. Maybe that's what I needed to do if I wanted to stay out of Ashland's head. Since I could not turn my dream catching off, I needed to learn how to focus on using it productively.

It seemed like a good idea at the time.

Chapter Two—Delilah

Another hot summer day passed by without a single customer darkening the door of the Iverson Sundries Store. A small, greasy-faced child plastered his face on the front glass of the store before he was shooed away by his rotund mother, but that was the closest thing to a customer we had. A stray cat had made his way in the back door, which I'd absently left open, but I showed him the way out with the help of one of my new Shoemaker brooms. Around 4 o'clock, after sweeping the floors for the third time, counting spools of thread and repeatedly climbing the ladder to check the top shelf of my stock, I gave up. Miss Page had been true to her word. Nobody wanted to have anything to do with me or my business. For weeks I had managed to ignore the hisses and unfriendly faces, but now it was all too much. Mobilians had clearly cast their vote for the respectable Claudette Page. Friendless, hopeless and feeling defeated, I decided to call it a day. It was sad to say, but even the newly arriving northerners avoided my store. It was a hard pill to swallow.

In contrast, Adam's woodworking business continued to increase—there was never a lack of activity at his shop. It took hard work to get it moving; I had to give him credit for that. In the beginning nobody had wanted to give him a chance either, but he'd been persistent. And it didn't hurt that he had a handsome face and friendly demeanor. Funny how nobody wanted to have anything to do with me, but my "brother" was perfectly acceptable. But then again, he wasn't an illegitimate bastard, a social usurper. What would my parents say about all this? What would I say to them?

I strolled down the wooden sidewalk, making a right turn toward Adam's shop—I was happy to make the turn off Dauphin Street away from the snooty shoppers who crowded every store but mine.

With a tinge of bitterness, I recalled this morning's conversation with the only other Iverson in this town. "It seems to me that Mobile has far too many aspiring female woodworkers. For God's sake, Adam, don't encourage them."

"What am I supposed to do, Delilah? Close the shop door and forbid anyone to walk inside without your permission? You cannot tell me you're worried about a few silly girls. You know only you have my heart."

We rarely spoke openly about how we felt about one another, and I was beginning to think that he was doing so now only to prevent further argument. Any other time he did not want to talk about our future together, or love, or feelings—except after the lamp blew out. I welcomed the guilt that came with the memory of our first time together. It had been awkward but wonderful until the sunlight streamed into the room and I woke up alone. He barely spoke to me in the days that followed, but he could not keep up the isolation since we lived in the same apartment above the store.

Well, I only had myself to blame. I loved a man who most of the county considered my brother. For the hundredth time I asked myself, "What was I trying to prove?" It's not like I needed money—both Dr. Page and my parents had been generous in their bequests to me—but I enjoyed working in the shop. It was the only life I knew, and now Claudette Page had seemingly put an end to all that. Mounting pressure from the unofficial leader of the local moral society had taken its toll.

The afternoon heat rolled up from the sidewalk like an unseen blanket. I suddenly missed the coolness of Canada; even my unfriendly cousins were not as cruel as Mobile society. Unwilling to witness their collective disdain any longer, I kept my eyes on the path in front of me until I crashed into another pedestrian. My victim was a young woman, slightly taller than me but wearing more fashionable attire than mine—a moss-green dress that flattered her wide gray eyes. Despite her otherwise polished appearance, she had a bundle of tight curly red hair that appeared barely controlled by a diamond-shaped green hat. Before I could mumble an apology and continue on my way, she said, "Miss Iverson? Adam Iverson's sister?"

"I am Delilah. May I help you?"

"Your brother tells me you are an excellent dressmaker. I happen to be in need of an excellent dressmaker." She rocked back on her heels delightedly, as if she were doing me the greatest favor imaginable by offering me a job. The young lady appeared oblivious to the stir our collision had caused. When I did not respond immediately she added, "Oh, my manners. My name is Maundy Weaver. I own the dress shop two streets over." She stuck her lace-gloved hand out to me, and I shook it.

"I had no idea my brother made a habit of visiting dress shops. Thank you, but I don't need a job." I tried to get by her, but she touched my arm.

"If I could have just a minute of your time. Would you join me for a glass of something cool?"

She quietly added, "My shop is just a minute away."

I was curious now, so I nodded and followed behind this mysterious Maundy Weaver. Her shop was indeed just two minutes away. I was surprised I had never seen it, but then again I had not spent much time exploring the area. I wondered how well my "brother" knew the woman and why she believed I needed a job. With a polite smile, she opened the side door and we stepped into a small parlor. She waved me to a seat at a polished two-person table. I recognized the work—Adam had built this. As Miss Weaver poured us a glass of something that looked like iced tea, I looked about me. Through an adjoining door I could see into her store. She had customers, busy dressmakers and an endless sea of colorful fabrics neatly arranged along the walls. In her parlor there was no evidence of her dressmaking business. However, I could see that she was fond of pink roses for her china, and many decorations displayed that painted theme.

"I am glad I caught you. When it gets this hot out, many shops close early. I suppose you find this climate a bit oppressive after Canada." She placed the glass in front of me, and I could not resist taking a sip. The drink was not tea at all but something much more delicious. She laughed at my reaction. "Sarsaparilla. I like the flavor, don't you?"

"Yes, I do. I see quite a bit of Adam's handiwork here in your parlor. I didn't know you were a customer, but I think there's some mistake. I'm not looking for a job.

As you know, I have my own store. Iverson Sundries on Dauphin Street."

"Miss Iverson, if I may be direct?" I nodded slowly. "I know all about your story and would like to help."

"Really? How much of my story do you think you know?" I set the glass down and stood. How dare Adam talk to this woman about our private matters!

"Please, sit. I am a woman who appreciates the direct approach. I did not mean to offend you; it's just that I too have crossed swords with Claudette. I know what a vicious adversary she can be, but you can beat her."

"So you think closing my store and coming to work for you as a dressmaker will beat her? I'm afraid I don't follow your logic." I sat back down, suddenly feeling tired.

"Of course you don't. You have no idea who I am or what I can do, Miss Iverson—or do you prefer Miss Page?"

"Delilah will do fine."

"I have just learned that your attorney, Mr. Peyton, has every intention of advising you to withdraw your case."

I could not hide my shock. "He can't do that!"

She laughed dryly. "Oh yes, he can. He's her cousin— and yours since you are a Page too. And as such, you can take him to court. You may not get much, but it will be on record and that might come in handy later. He should've shared with you his connection with her at your first meeting. It's what legal folks call a 'conflict of interest.'" I sank back in the chair. Could this day get any worse? Miss Weaver seemed to pick up on my thoughts. "Are you ready to quit?" She removed her hat pin and her hat and tossed it on the table beside her. She didn't attempt to tame her wild red hair as she leaned toward me with one arm on the table, waiting for my answer.

"I don't quit so easily. Why does my situation interest you so much, Ms. Weaver?"

With a smile she answered me, "Maundy, please. Why shouldn't it? You're a woman. I'm a woman. I believe we women should stick together. This world is an unfriendly place for us, hence my offer. I am not merely offering you a job; I offer you a way to get even. You need something—and you need it very badly. I can help you get it."

Her tone of voice made the fine hairs on the back of my neck stand up. "And what is it you think I need?" The thought that I should never cross this woman flashed through my mind.

She laughed again. "The only thing a woman ever really needs—information."

Surprised by her answer, I asked, "Information? I don't understand. Information about dressmaking?"

"Don't tell me you're dull, Delilah. You can't be dull with that face. No, not dressmaking. You'd be surprised how much you can learn during a dress fitting. There are not many social situations in which the classes mingle so easily. I have been a dressmaker all my life, as my mother was before me and hers before her. None of us Weaver women got into the business because we loved dresses." She cackled at some joke that only she knew. "With just a glance I can take your measurements and see the perfect dress for you or any woman—tall, thin, short, fat. I can make any woman look and feel good. With that ability comes a lot of trust. Women trust me. And when they trust you, they tell you things."

"And what kind of things do I need to hear?"

"Everyone has a secret, and most people don't want those secrets to see the light of day. That includes the high-and-mighty Claudette Page. In fact, I would venture to say that of all the people in the great city of Mobile, she has the biggest secret of all." She sipped her sarsaparilla and smiled at me through her yellow-tinged teeth.

"What secret might that be?"

"Oh, that's for you to figure out. I don't like Claudette Page, but she is not my mortal enemy—she's yours. Your very existence has threatened everything she holds dear. Her reputation, her wealth, her family's name— these are all things she's willing to die for. But if you find out her secret and confront her with it, she'll slink away like a scolded puppy. Now," she said, setting her glass down and smoothing her dress as she stood, "I need a dressmaker. Your business is in shambles, and that's not likely to change. Put a sign on the door that says you're closed for remodeling. Have your brother install some new cabinets or something. While he works on that project, you come help me. I'll make sure you get the opportunity to get the information you need."

"Why are you helping me? I'm not ungrateful, but why?"

"I'll keep my reasons to myself for now, if you don't mind. It's not that I don't trust you, but I would like to wait. Work for me for the next six weeks, and I can promise you everything will be different."

I stood up and extended my hand to her. "You have yourself a deal, Maundy."

She shook it and smiled broadly. "Smart girl. I'm Miss Weaver during working hours. I'll see you at Rose Cottage in the morning."

"At your house? I thought I was to work here, in the shop?"

"Oh no, dear. This little shop is for regular folks like you and me. My most exclusive clients have their fittings and consultations at Rose Cottage. It's a private service that I offer them. For example, I have clients who need help with their Mardi Gras ball dresses, but privacy is an issue. Keeping those dresses secret is a must until the big reveal at the ball. It's kind of a local tradition. It's ridiculous how they try to outdo one another, but if it's pearls they want, it's pearls they will get. Or whatever strikes their fancy. That's not going to be a problem for you, is it?"

"Not at all. And where is Rose Cottage located?"

"Turn left on Monterey Street and follow it to Virginia Street. My house is behind the Magnolia Cemetery. You can't miss it. It's the yellow two-story with the green shutters. Do you have a carriage?"

"Yes, I do."

"Bring it. It will rain tomorrow. It always rains after heat like this. And dress nicely, Miss Page. You'll meet your new attorney tomorrow."

"New attorney?"

"My friend, Jackson Keene. He'll help you get all this sorted out."

"I don't know how to thank you for all this."

"One day I'll tell you." She leaned forward and peered into my eyes. "One day I will ask you for a favor. I will expect you to grant it. In the meantime, keep your eyes and ears open and your mouth closed. Don't ask questions. The quieter, the less intrusive you are, the more likely they'll trust you and the sooner you'll hear something. Something useful you can use to put that old woman in her place. I have had enough of her and her moral society."

With a final handshake I slipped out of the house and walked back home. In one conversation I had lost everything and gained it all again. I wondered about my new partner, Maundy Weaver. What did she want from me? It would do no good to ask. I could tell she was not the kind of woman who would be easily persuaded to do anything other than what she wanted. Still, this was better than any plan I currently had. Once again, life had handed me an unexpected fork in the road. I hoped this time I had chosen the right path.

Chapter Three—Henri

I drizzled the bourbon into the hot pan and watched the flames appear. I worked the pan just like a short-order cook, coating the pecans in the decadent glaze. Turning off the flame, I continued to cook the alcohol out, pleased that I hadn't burned the pecans. At least not this batch. Glancing at my wristwatch, I had a moment of panic—Detra Ann would arrive any minute, and I wanted everything to be perfect. I did not want to stop and think about what I was doing, how foolish I was to even dream that Detra Ann and I would ever be anything more than friends. But I did hope and dream. Although I couldn't deny that I cared about her, I didn't know how she felt about me. Not only that, but we were business partners. What was I doing having heart palpitations over a business partner? "Strike one, strike two," as my granddad used to say.

Walking the pan to the dining room table, I spooned the glaze over the plated roasted chicken. I couldn't help but smile and for a moment felt confident that at least she'd like the dish I'd prepared for her. I tossed my dirty apron across the bar in the kitchen and searched for my lighter. No, on second thought, lighting candles would be coming on too strong. With nervous hands, I struggled to open a stubborn bottle of wine when I heard an unusual noise coming from the direction of the bathroom. It sounded like squirrels scratching at the wall—or someone breaking in! I put the wine aside and slipped quietly into my office. Removing my gun from the desk drawer, I went down the hall to investigate the source of the noise. I paused in the hallway waiting to hear the sound again. I was much more agile than I had been a year ago. I'd spent so much time at the gym—I had never been this fit before. My thirty-fifth birthday was last week, and I hadn't told a soul. I didn't need to be reminded how old I was. I couldn't turn back time, but I could get in shape. And I had.

Scratch, scratch...

Nope, the noise wasn't coming from the bathroom. It was coming from the guest room. As I stepped toward the door, I cocked my gun. I stood sweating in my gold-colored polo shirt, silently counting backwards from three. I heard a thud on the other side of the door and swung it open, my gun poised and ready to shoot the invader.

"Get up now!" I shouted in my most authoritative voice. "On your feet! Put your hands where I can see them!"

The intruder didn't respond right away, but when she did I almost fell over. "Calm down, Henri. It's just me," the crumpled figure complained.

"Lenore?"

"Yep, the one and only."

"What the hell are you doing climbing through the window? I could have shot you!"

"If you shoot me, you better hope you kill me. Because if you didn't, you know I would kick your ass!" She dusted herself off and stood up to face me. Her expression let me know that nothing much had changed. She was still as crazy and defiant as ever.

From the way her clothing looked, she didn't need to bother trying to tidy herself up. The only time I'd seen my cousin dressed appropriately or nicely was at our grandmother's funeral, and that had been more than twenty years ago. Today's outfit was red leggings and an oversize pink shirt with black combat boots.

"I'm going to ask again, why are you climbing through my window? You plan on robbing me?"

"I don't want nothing you have, Henri Devecheaux—I never have, and I'm sure as hell not a thief!" A little more apologetically she added, "I couldn't come through the front door. You got a damn ghost on the front porch. You know I don't fool with no ghosts."

I laughed, setting my gun down with a sigh of relief. "What do you mean?" Before I could get an answer from her, the doorbell rang. "Um...just wait right here."

"No, Henri! Don't you open that door! I'm telling you the truth, fool! Don't you ever listen? A ghost is out there!"

"Lenore, have you been drinking? That's my dinner guest, Detra Ann. She's a real person, my business partner—not a ghost." I sighed and pointed toward the screwed-up window. "Just fix my screen. Please. I'll be right back." I couldn't believe my luck. My crazy cousin had to show up tonight of all nights. Once again I felt as if the Man Upstairs had it in for me.

Sliding the gun into the back of my pants, I strode to the front door. It wouldn't do to wave a gun around in front of Detra Ann, considering she'd been shot last year. The glass reflected her slender frame. I could tell from the length of her shadow that she was wearing high heels. That was promising. You didn't wear high heels unless you wanted to impress someone. At least that was true for most women I'd met. On the other hand, Detra Ann wore high heels almost every day. I wasn't sure who she was trying to impress. She was a natural beauty, even with bleached blond hair.

I opened the door with a smile, trying to act as naturally as possible. "Hey! Right on time. Come in, please."

"Oh, Henri. It smells wonderful. Nice shirt." She kissed my cheek and handed me a bottle of her favorite red wine. I pretended I didn't notice the smell of whiskey on her breath. "I hope this goes with what you've prepared." She flashed an empty smile.

"This is perfect." Remembering the gun in my waistband, I pointed to the dining room and excused myself. "Make yourself at home. I'll be right back."

"Are you still fussing in the kitchen? Is there something I can help you with?"

"No. Everything is ready. This won't take a minute."

"Okey dokey." She smiled again and walked to the dining room.

As I was returning the gun to the desk drawer, I heard the shower running in the bathroom. What was I going to do with Lenore? She had always been a lost soul, but her behavior had gotten worse after Aleezabeth disappeared. We had been the three amigos—Peas,

Carrots and Onions, our grandma had called us. I was pretty sure I'd been Onions.

Aleezabeth…

How long had it been since I'd summoned up her memory? When was the last time I'd called the sheriff of Dumont and demanded an update? Too long ago. I'd let Aleezabeth down, first by leaving her to walk home by herself and now by failing to find her and bring her home.

I leaned against the doorframe with the wine bottle in my hand. So much for a nice, relaxing evening with Detra Ann. I'd have to explain Lenore before she had a chance to crash our dinner.

"Hey, you coming? I'm going to start without you!"

"Yep, on the way." I stopped by the kitchen for the corkscrew and strolled into join her. To my surprise, Detra Ann had lit the candles and was already digging into supper. I poured the wine and sat down with her.

"Hidden talents, Henri. I had no idea you could cook like this. Are you professionally trained? Did you go to culinary school somewhere?"

I took a big swig of the fruity red wine. "No, but I've always loved cooking. I think it's just a part of my heritage. You know, everyone from New Orleans can cook."

She shook her head as she finished a bite of the chicken. "That's not true at all. I had an aunt from New Orleans, and she was the worst cook on the planet.

Every Christmas she'd make us these God-awful pralines and then call us the next day to see if we'd eaten them. It was so funny because my dad would lie to her and tell her they hit the spot. She never knew he had a hole dug in the backyard that he lovingly called 'the spot.'"

"That sounds like something my father would have done. He was kind of a jokester."

"I've never heard you talk about your father. Is he still alive?"

I took another swig of wine and eyed the hallway nervously. "I'm not sure."

"What?" she asked incredulously.

"He kind of slipped away. Daddy liked playing music, or he did before he hooked up with my mother. He was a high school science teacher, but he dabbled in music—mostly jazz. One weekend a group of his old band buddies came around, and when they left town, Dad and his sax left too. I assumed he left with them."

"That must have been so hard on you. How old were you?"

"Fourteen. My birthday was the month before he left."

"And you've never seen him in all this time?"

"No, but that's not unusual for my family—we're all a bunch of wanderers. For example, my cousin Lenore showed up tonight. I haven't seen her in years, and suddenly she's here."

Her dark eyelashes fluttered in surprise. "You should have said something. We could have had dinner another night. I hope I didn't inconvenience you, Henri."

"You're never an inconvenience."

She dabbed her mouth with the linen napkin and smirked. I could tell she didn't believe me. After a year, I knew her facial expressions pretty well. At least I thought I did. We chitchatted about work stuff, like the crate of antiques that had come in that morning, a client that refused to pay us, the noise from the construction on Dauphin Street. When our plates were nearly empty and the conversation died down, I felt more relaxed. I was pretty sure that Lenore had passed out on my bed, but at least she wouldn't be crashing our dinner date—I hoped.

"I have to admit I had an ulterior motive for inviting you here."

She set the napkin on the table, leaned back in the chair and appraised me suspiciously. "Not to steal your thunder, but before you tell me, I have something for you. For your birthday."

"How did you know I had a birthday?"

"I took a peek at your driver's license a while back. Since you didn't mention it, I figured you wanted to keep it quiet. You know, thirty-five isn't ancient." Opening her oversize purse she removed a gold box with a royal blue ribbon wrapped around it. "This is for you." She slid it toward me.

I laughed in surprise. "I can't believe you did that. You're full of surprises, Detra Ann."

"Wait until you open it."

I picked up the box and put it back down. "I am sure this is a wonderful gift, but I really want something else."

She froze for a second and said, "Okay, what do you want?"

"I want a dance. I mean, it is my birthday." I walked to the CD player and hit play. I hadn't planned this, but it felt right. Etta James began her sweet serenade.

At last...my love has come along...my lonely days are over...and life is like a song...

With a sad smile, Detra Ann joined me on the makeshift dance floor. Her arms slid around my neck, and I held her close. Her long blond hair rubbed against my hands, and I did my best to breathe slowly so my heart wouldn't beat out of my chest.

"Remember that day, at the ribbon-cutting?"

"Yes, I remember," I said quietly. I knew it was hard for her to talk about TD, even now.

"I don't know what I would have done if I had looked out into that audience and didn't see you."

"You would have been just fine, Detra Ann. You are strong—stronger than you think."

She squeezed me tighter and laid her head on my shoulder. I couldn't help but touch her hair. "I will never forget it." We danced until Etta sang her last notes. When the dance ended, she stepped back and reached for the gift before I could say or do anything else. "Now open it before I change my mind."

Quickly, I opened it, pulling the ribbon first and removing the golden cardboard lid. Inside was a silver key tied to another blue ribbon. I recognized it—this was the key to Cotton City Treasures. Puzzled, I turned it over in my hand.

"I'm giving you my share of the business, Henri. It's time for me to move on. I've taken a job in Atlanta—I'm leaving at the end of the week."

It felt like someone had kicked me in the gut. I put the key back in the box and replaced the lid. "I can't take this. This is too much, Detra Ann. I can't let you do this."

"It's already done, my friend. I signed the papers yesterday, and it is official. You are the sole proprietor of Cotton City Treasures—you own it all. It's just my way of saying thank you. If it weren't for you, I wouldn't be here today. I mean, I know I'm not a hundred percent yet, but you have been a lifesaver. Truly. Thank you for everything."

Stunned, I murmured, "You're welcome."

She sprang from her chair and hugged me, and I breathed in her sweet smell. Detra Ann sometimes wore expensive perfume, the kind you normally only got a whiff of in fashion magazines, but then there were times when she smelled like sun-dried sheets and wildflowers. That's how I always thought of her. And now she was leaving. "I thought this would be easy, but it's not. I will miss you most of all," she whispered in my ear. After a few moments, she reached for her purse and headed out the door. "I have to go. I'll come by and see you before I leave, I promise."

I watched her car lights disappear down Conception Street, and then I closed the door. I felt like my heart had been snatched out. Lenore was standing in the doorway, her hair wild and damp from her shower. Her olive-colored skin practically glowed in the candlelight.

"Please tell me you weren't intending on telling that ghost you loved her. She's not for you, Henri."

"You don't know what you're talking about, Lenore."

She clucked her tongue, "You've always been a fool when it came to women. Remember Peaches?" As she strolled across the wooden floor, I noticed she was wearing a pair of my socks. She peered through the blinds and said, "She was a nightmare, and she left you high and dry just like I told you she would. Then there was that red-haired stripper, Anastasia..."

"She wasn't a stripper—she was a burlesque dancer, and that was over ten years ago."

"Don't correct me. You've got a bad habit of thinking you're the only one that's right, Henri Lamar Devecheaux. You can't love that girl. She's already dead—she's a ghost. At the very least, she's a shade."

"What are you talking about?" I knew I would regret asking, but I did it anyway. "What the hell is a shade, Lenore?"

"Someone who's been touched by Death. A part of her is already gone. Death only got his bony hands on part of her, but all that's left is a shadow—a shade. He'll come for the rest." She stood closer to me now—she touched my hand tentatively as if she thought I was a shade too. "You know what I am saying is true. I can see it in your face. What do you have to do with this, Henri?" I didn't answer her. I wanted her to leave my home, but I was too polite to say so. She touched my arm again. Sure that I was real, her face softened; her voice was unusually soft and kind. "She's someone who should have died but escaped the reaper's hands. But he'll come back for her. And if you're anywhere around her when he does, he might take you too. She's been amongst the dead, seen them, touched them. Death won't let her go—she's his. She can never be yours, cousin."

"I don't believe a word you're saying. You don't either. You just like tormenting me, don't you? This isn't about Detra Ann at all. This is about Aleezabeth. Tell me the truth, Lenore. Why are you here? What do you want? Money?"

As if she didn't hear me, she walked around the room, examining my pictures and my collection of antique silver spoons. "That's probably why she's drinking and taking those pills. She feels cold Death creeping into her bones and thinks she can escape it. It won't work. It never does. She's a ghost already…"

"Shut up, Lenore! If you don't stop talking like that, you will have to go. I don't believe Detra Ann is the only one drinking too much. You're on dope now, aren't you?"

She closed her eyes and held her breath, tilting her head like she was listening to an invisible voice. Then her eyes sprung open and she said, "I'm here to help you, Henri. I didn't come for any other reason. You're about to see the supernatural like you've never seen it before! I want to help you, cousin. You're the last family I got, and I'll be damned if I just let you go." She pursed her lips and scowled at me. "I lost Aleezabeth. We both lost her—I won't lose you too. I am staying right here until that ghost is gone. Have a care for your soul, Henri. Please."

I rubbed my forehead in frustration. "Listen, if you want to stay for a while, fine. But there are some ground rules. Number one, you aren't just lying around the house all day. You've got to get a job. When I leave the house, you leave the house. No climbing in the windows or kicking down doors. Number two, you leave Detra Ann alone. No talking to her about all this crazy stuff—in fact, you don't talk to her at all. She's been through enough. Number three, if you steal from me, you're out of here. All I have to do is call Detective Simmons at the Mobile Police Department and she'll come pick you up *tout de suite*. Those are the rules. You understand?"

Lenore could see I was serious. She didn't argue and nodded her head. "Can I smoke in here?"

"Not in my house, but there's a chair in the backyard if you want to puff on your cancer sticks. You've got the guest room—that's the room you broke into. Do you have clothes?"

"I've got enough, and the guest room suits me fine."

"I'm cleaning the kitchen and going to bed. There's some leftover chicken in there if you're hungry."

"I think I'll go smoke first." Without even a thank you, Lenore slipped out of the house and into the darkened backyard.

With a sigh I went to the kitchen to tidy up. Corking the wine and removing the dishes from the table, I slid on my rubber gloves and let the hot water run in the sink. I had a dishwasher, a nice stainless steel one, but I liked washing dishes by hand. It was therapeutic. After tonight's turn of events, I needed some therapy. The woman I loved—yes, I could admit that now—was leaving me behind. *Isn't that terrific?* I cracked the window a bit to let some cool air in. It was too early in the year to turn on the air conditioning, but the house felt stuffy tonight.

I squirted the blue dishwashing liquid into the sink and watched the suds build. I caught a whiff of Lenore's cigarette. I thought about asking her to move away from the window, but then I heard her whisper into a phone. "Hey! You ain't going to believe this, but I found one." I froze and turned off the water. It was quiet for a moment. "Sure I'm sure." Another pause. "Yeah, probably, but we'll have to move fast."

Chills ran up and down my spine. For a second it was as if the air stopped moving and I stopped breathing. I knew exactly what—no, who—Lenore was talking about.

Detra Ann.

Chapter Four—Carrie Jo

Desmond Taylor insisted that I meet him at Idlewood first thing in the morning, and I was happy to do so. Off the beaten path, the old house stood off Carlen Street about a mile from Seven Sisters. Another forgotten gem crumbling into the Mobile landscape, Idlewood was in nowhere near the condition Ashland's family home had been. It was in far worse shape. And to think I believed restoring Seven Sisters had been challenging. Still, the old house had good bones, as Terrence Dale used to say. And to top it off, it had a fascinating history. One that I couldn't walk away from.

Idlewood was actually a twin home. The original house was the Idlewild Plantation in Derby, Louisiana. The McClellans visited the home and loved it so much they purchased copies of the original plans and reconstructed it here in Mobile. Idlewild was a raised plantation—a unique construction because of its mix of French and English features. Typical for the wild woods of Louisiana, it had been a rarity during its time here in Mobile. The front facade of Idlewood had three dormers, which gave it a graceful look despite the sagging roof. Rusty, ornamental cast-iron balustrades looked promising but in much need of some skilled attention. But the thing I loved the most were the galleries. This type of house normally had molded capitals, but Idlewood's galleries were lined with gorgeous fluted, Doric columns that begged to be restored to their former elegance.

According to Mr. Taylor, Idlewood's current owner, this Greek revival plantation house had undergone at least a dozen changes since the original construction.

But fortunately these had been relatively minor and had not taken away from the original owner's vision. Luckily for me, I knew what Idlewood had really looked like, right down to the paisley wallpaper in the hallway—I had seen it in a dream. Once upon a time, about a hundred and fifty years ago, there had been a grand Christmas ball held here at Idlewood. Dr. Hoyt Page and his beloved Christine Cottonwood rekindled their romance in the upstairs nursery. A little boy battled the flu, and rare Christmas snowflakes had fallen, much to the delight of a pair of cocker spaniels and the gathered party. Unfortunately, I could not revisit the nursery or any of the rooms on the top floor, as the stairs were deemed unsafe.

"Tell me, Mr. Taylor, what did you have in mind?"

The older man thought carefully before he spoke. "I'll be honest with you, Mrs. Stuart. I am not sure what to do with this old house. It doesn't seem practical to me to restore it. My wife and the Historical Society seem to think differently, but then again my wife is a sentimental old gal." He chuckled and continued, "I don't have a bottomless pocketbook, but I do have a heart to restore Idlewood, if that's possible. From what I hear about your work at Seven Sisters, you really put that home back on the map. Maybe we can do that here. I don't know. Believe it or not, I've been offered a substantial grant to begin the restoration. But I'm not a foolish man. I've been in business all my life, and I know this kind of project isn't something to take too lightly. We could be looking at a very long project, and I have a construction business to run. I don't have time to manage all this. Not to mention I wouldn't know where to start."

I chewed my lip and looked around the room at the dusty walls and cracked floors. He was right, of course. Restoration was hard work. It took hundreds of hours of research, and then there were acquisitions. Then there was the reconstruction of the property and meeting all the requirements of the local historical society, which could be a major task in itself. I felt sad thinking about working on a new project without Terrence Dale—and probably without Ashland. Still, this was what I did. What I had always wanted to do. Maybe getting the Seven Sisters job *had* been just a fluke—I'm sure Hollis Matthews knew about my dream catching from Mia, and that's why they wanted me in Mobile—but this…this was an opportunity to prove my abilities as a researcher.

"You are right. It is a commitment, Mr. Taylor. Here's how we'll start. Let me ask you a few questions."

After another thirty minutes I got the bottom line. Mr. Taylor didn't want to be involved in the daily decisions, but he did want monthly updates. He would use his construction company to do the work under my team's supervision. Before anything began or any plans were finalized, we would undertake a lengthy appraisal process. He had a dollar figure in mind, and he wouldn't pursue the restoration if the cost exceeded that amount. His ultimate goal was for the home to turn enough profit so all future maintenance would be self-supported. He didn't want to be stuck managing a "money pit," and I couldn't blame him there.

And one more caveat. He had no idea how to collect antiques, but his wife was eager to help. In fact, he wanted her to help. I agreed to his terms, and we ended the meeting with a handshake. Mr. and Mrs. Taylor were going out of town on an extended cruise in a few days, and he wanted to have a detailed project proposal before he left. Which meant I'd have to work day and night for the next forty-eight hours to pull something together. I agreed to do that but reminded him this was just a preliminary proposal. When it came to restoration, there was always that one thing you hadn't considered—like the cost of taking care of any bodies you uncovered.

I left the meeting so excited that my hands were shaking as I dug my cell phone out of my purse. Ashland should have been the first person I called, but after last night, I still couldn't face him. I thought about calling Rachel and then just frowned in the rearview mirror and tossed the phone back in my purse.

You are being a total jerk, Carrie Jo! You can't get mad about some dreams.

Oh, yeah? Well, why is he dreaming about other women? Is he seeing other women?

Sick of my own drama, I flipped on the radio. Bob Marley sang "Three Little Birds," and for the next fifteen minutes I tapped my fingers on the steering wheel as I sang loudly and completely off-key. By the time I made it to my office at Oak Plaza, I felt more like my old self again.

The first thing I saw when I stepped inside was a ridiculously large vase full of pink roses. There had to have been at least a hundred buds crammed into the white ceramic vase. It smelled glorious, but it did seem a bit much. Unless you were at a funeral. As I slid my coat off, I smiled at Rachel. "Gee, who died? Those can't be from Chip."

"Uh, no. Those are for you, actually." She handed me a card and smiled. "Happy anniversary!"

"Oh." I took the card and smiled sheepishly. "Thank you so much."

"You hit the flower jackpot, I think. I'd be lucky if Chip bought me just a half dozen. He's a sweetie but not big on sentimentalism. Me either, I guess. What should I do with these? Put them in your office? I can't leave them here. I don't think the visitors will be able to see my desk."

"I'll take them. I have a table in my office. Let me put my purse and coat away first. Then I'll tell you the awesome news!"

"No bother. I think I can handle this monster." Rachel wrapped her arms around the massive vase. "So what did you get Ashland?"

I felt a bit woozy for a second but caught my balance easily. I wished I could tell Rachel my secret, but I had to tell Ashland first. If I ever got around to speaking to him again. Just a few weeks ago I thought telling Ashland that we were having a baby would be the perfect anniversary present. Now I didn't know when I would tell him. "I'll be honest with you. I've been so busy with our new office that I haven't even thought about it."

"Carrie Jo! Are you kidding me? It's your second anniversary—you have to do *something*." As if she could fix my problem, she asked, "What did you give him last year?"

"Okay, now who's being sentimental?" I helped her position the white ceramic vase on the table and arranged the flowers. Touching the soft petals, I remembered our first kiss. I would never forget that night. It seemed like a lifetime ago.

"Let's see…last year I got him a first-edition copy of *The Jungle Book*, believe it or not. He's a huge Kipling fan."

Shoot! I must be the worst wife on the planet. Spying on his dreams and forgetting our anniversary. Yep, I'm batting a thousand.

Before she could ask me anything else, I told her the good news about Idlewood. Immediately we fired up our computers and began grabbing the research we needed for the proposal. Of course, we had the Seven Sisters model to go by, but each job had its own challenges. Ashland called me sometime around lunch, but I let it go to voicemail. Rachel's eyes widened, but she didn't ask any more questions. We ordered Chinese and kept working. By the time five o'clock came around, I needed a break from numbers and plans and debated on whether or not to head home.

Just then, Chip arrived to pick up Rachel. I'd already asked her to work on a Saturday, and I couldn't very well insist she work past five. She had a life—it wasn't her fault I was trying to avoid mine. "Have fun, you two."

Chip waved goodbye and walked out the door, but Rachel lingered behind. "Carrie Jo, it's your anniversary. Go home, for goodness' sake. Whatever you two are going through, you can work it out. I just know it. We've got a handle on this now. Go home. I'll come and help you tomorrow."

"I appreciate that. I'll go home soon, I promise."

"No need, apparently...your husband is here! Have a nice night! Don't do anything I wouldn't do."

"Which is what?" I asked with a laugh.

Ashland walked in, his expensive cologne filling the room before his arrival. God, that man always smelled so good. And he looked great, of course. I could see he'd bought a new shirt, light blue like his eyes, and he had taken the time to get a haircut. My emotions surged again—on one hand I wanted to feel his hands on my skin, but on the other hand I wanted to slap the smile off his face. This was indeed a dilemma.

Where had even-tempered, reasonable Carrie Jo gone? When would she be back?

"Hey, I tried to call you. Did you get my messages?"

"Were there more than one?" I picked up my cell and saw he'd called three times. "Oh yeah, I've been slammed here. It's been kind of crazy. Sorry about that." I shuffled the papers around on my desk and avoided eye contact.

"You haven't been in business for more than a week. You're slammed already? What do you have going on?" He sounded a little irritated, as if he didn't quite believe me. He picked up the sheaf of papers on my desk and scanned them. A slow smile spread across his handsome face. "You got Idlewood? That's amazing, Carrie Jo."

Snatching the papers away from him I answered hotly, "I haven't got anything yet. I'm working on the proposal, and I have less than forty eight hours to get it to Desmond Taylor. This might be my only chance to work on the Idlewood restoration. I don't want to blow it."

"Oh, I see." He noticed the flowers on the side table and pointed to them. "You like the flowers?"

"Yes, they are very nice. Thank you, and happy anniversary. Your gift isn't here yet. It might be a few days late."

"Carrie Jo, what is going on? You've hardly talked to me all week. I get the feeling you're mad about something, but I don't know what. Please just tell me what's on your mind."

"I don't have time for this right now, Ashland." I added more gently, "When I finish this proposal I swear we'll talk all you want. Okay?"

"Fine, Why not let me help you? I'll cancel the dinner reservations I made, and we'll work on this together. Who else, besides you, knows more about restoration projects than me? What are you in the mood for?

Chinese? Italian? I could call Mama's and go pick up something."

The idea of food made my stomach feel queasy. All I wanted was a bottle of water and some oranges. I'd always heard that pregnant women had strange cravings—I didn't want much of anything except oranges. I couldn't get enough citrus fruit lately.

"Are you okay? You look a little pale."

"Yes, I'm fine. I've just been staring at these computer screens all day. You don't have to stay, Ashland. I am sure you're just as tired as I am. Go home—I'll be there in a couple of hours." I sat behind my desk and didn't wait for an answer.

"Damn it, CJ! It's our anniversary! Can't you at least pretend you want to spend it with me?"

Leaping out of the chair I yelled back at him, "Can't you give me some space?"

"Tell me what's going on!" His voice grew louder and I could tell by his body language that he was none too happy with me. I couldn't deny he'd been patient about the proposal, but I still couldn't shake the feeling of betrayal.

"Alright! You want to know so much." I flew to my feet. "You've been dreaming about women—lots and lots of women! You don't even care that I am lying right beside you! Every night it's someone new, Ash. I can't remember the last time I got to sleep without being forced to watch my husband make love to someone else! You tell *me* what the hell is going on!"

"Are you seriously mad about some dream? Like I get to pick what I dream about? Is this really what you're mad about, Carrie Jo?" He laughed bitterly and put his hands on his hips. "All this time I thought I'd done something wrong, and this is why you're pissed? I can't believe what I'm hearing!"

"You better believe it!" Fat, salty tears welled up in my eyes. I felt another wave of nausea. "Why are you all of a sudden dreaming about other women? Are you having an affair? With that brunette you're fantasizing about?"

"Who? What the heck are you talking about—I don't even know how to answer that. You know…" He raised his hands and walked toward the door. "When you're done being crazy, call me."

I stared in shock as he walked out the door, making sure to slam it behind him. I fell back in my seat and cried my eyes out. He was right, I was acting crazy. What the heck was wrong with me? I suddenly missed Bette. I needed someone to talk to, someone who could help me navigate this ball of confusion that I'd wound myself up in. Detra Ann had quietly stepped out of my life, and Rachel and I didn't have the kind of relationship that I felt comfortable sharing my problems with her. Most people had a mother to talk to. Not me.

Ugh, I don't have time to feel sorry for myself. I wiped my face with a tissue and continued to work on my project. Work was probably the best thing for me right now. If I were home, I would just wallow in my misery. At least at work I could focus on something else. I struggled with the spreadsheets for about an hour and then gave up. My mind wasn't here, and neither was my heart. I wasn't going to get anything done tonight except cry all over my paperwork. I grabbed my purse, hoping Ashland had gone home. He was right, we did need to talk, and I would have to start with an apology. I got behind the wheel of my BMW, slid the key in the ignition and turned it.

Click, click.

And that made me cry too. After a few minutes, I rubbed my red face with my now soppy tissue and decided to walk home. At least I'd get some fresh air and have time to rehearse what I would say. It was only four blocks from the office, and I hadn't worn heels. A light winter wind blew, but the temperatures were only in the fifties. It had been a long time since I'd gone for a walk through the streets of downtown Mobile. I thought about Seven Sisters and how hard it would be to get there. *No, you've got enough problems, Carrie Jo.* I kept my eye on the broken sidewalks and tried to enjoy the scenery. This was a particularly nice block, with lovely old homes and cast-iron fences with fleur de lis perching atop the occasional posts. I walked past a house with thumping music and excited young people. When was the last time I'd been to a party?

Halfway there now. Just ahead I saw the low-hanging sign that marked one of Mobile's most significant landmarks, the Magnolia Cemetery. Often referred to by locals as the City of the Dead, some of the city's earliest citizens were buried here, along with hundreds of Civil War soldiers. There were even huge mausoleums that housed the bones of entire generations of families. I approached the open gate and slowed my walk. I had always meant to explore this place but had never gotten around to it. I tugged my purse up on my shoulder as if some nefarious purse-snatcher hovered near me in the shadows of the great oak trees.

A flash of light caught my eye. *Must be the night watchman making rounds.* I paused at the open gate. *Hmm…that's odd. I thought they closed this place at dusk.* Well, I was here, and there was a good chance that Ashland would need some time to cool off. Shoving the squeaking gate open the rest of the way, I headed toward the light. I'd let the security guard know I was here, have a quick peek around and then head home. No harm done, right?

The light bounced through the trees, and it was difficult to keep up with it as I navigated the maze of graves. I hoped to avoid tripping over the roots of the massive oak and magnolia trees that littered the cemetery. I couldn't help but squint at the grave markers of some of the cemetery's older residents. Some of the tombstones were so old that the names were hard to read. Since the beginnings of Mobile, bodies had been laid to rest here—neatly at first, and then much more haphazardly as the centuries passed and space became an issue. Everywhere I looked I could see sentimental stonework like weeping angels and broken columns. Besides the children's markers, I found the broken columns the saddest. They represented the last person in a family line. During the Civil War there were a lot of broken columns installed in the Magnolia Cemetery. How many sons had died during that horrendous war?

This was no time to be distracted. Shaking myself out of my reverie, I called out to the security guard. "Hello! Excuse me!" The cemetery was getting darker by the second, and there were no lights besides the bouncing light I had chased from one side of the grounds to the other. Peering through the dim light, I tried to discern a figure. I stepped out from under an old oak covered in Spanish moss into a clearing and watched the light. The air suddenly felt thick and, for lack of a better word, sparkly. It occurred to me that what I was seeing was not normal at all. That wasn't a flashlight! What had appeared to be the beam of a flashlight suddenly changed color to a soft amber glow that bounced ever so softly off the ground about three feet.

"What in the world?" I thought perhaps it could be children or teenagers playing in the cemetery, but that didn't make sense either. I leaned against the oak and called one more time. I had to be imagining things. "Hello?" The light stopped bouncing, expanded and then shrank to half its original size. "Oh my God!"

Yep. This was something supernatural.

Suddenly the light shot across the cemetery toward the gate to the left. Without thinking, I took off after it. It didn't move as I got closer to the gate; it just hung in midair, still bouncing a little. I'd heard of orbs before but had never actually seen one. If that was what this was. Many people thought these were some type of ghost, but I had no idea. Most of the ghosts I saw were in dreams. Well, before Seven Sisters.

It was completely dark now and a chill crept into the air, a chill that had not been there before. Another warning sign. Clutching my purse, I ran ahead, stopping to hide behind a moldy mausoleum wall. I held my breath and silently counted to ten before slowly peering around the corner to take a peek at the light. The reasonable part of my brain told me to call someone, but who would that be? I watched as the light hovered in midair just this side of the gate. Maybe it wanted me to follow? Why else would it hang around?

I looked around the cemetery and saw no one else—no one living, anyway. I was by myself except for whatever entity this was I was chasing. Terrified, I leaned flush against the marble, the cold creeping through my clothing. I heard a noise I couldn't identify—it started as a low moan and quickly became a screech. A small, dark shadow launched itself from the top of the mausoleum and landed on the ground beside me. It was a damn cat! A gray cat with an attitude, upset at the invader who had appeared in his playground. After my heart stopped pounding in my chest, I peeked around the corner again and took a deep breath. It was now or never.

I stepped out quickly, as if I could surprise it. As I did, the light flared and passed through the closed gate, disappearing into the dark Alabama night. I decided to follow it—I'd come this far. The gate was stubborn and didn't give way without a fight. I gripped the cold cast-iron bars with both hands and pushed as hard as I could, and the gate swung open. I felt the chill again, and the hairs on my arms stood up.

Here I was again, completely surrounded by the supernatural with nowhere to run. Still clutching my purse like it was some sort of fashionable life preserver, I took a deep breath and stepped through the gate.

That was the last thing I remembered.

Chapter Five—Ashland

My wife never ceased to amaze me, but lately the surprises weren't anything good. To think she'd been spying on my dreams and accused me of cheating. I couldn't believe this was the Carrie Jo I loved and married. When I first saw her, she took my breath away. The more I got to know her, the more I was amazed at her knowledge, but it wasn't just that. She had a deep compassion for people, even though at times she doubted her own ability to help them.

I will always remember the first time I saw her—a beautiful woman standing at the foot of the stairs of my family home. She wore a red blouse with slightly puffy sleeves and a red and white skirt with a tiny rose pattern all over it. Her legs were tanned and lovely, her face even lovelier with amazing green eyes and wild curly hair. I could tell instantly that she had a sense of humor and that she would not be easily impressed with my southern-boy swagger.

Seeing her there that night was like a sign, or at least I thought it was. But now I didn't know what to think. I stuffed some clothing in my overnight bag and headed out the door. I didn't leave a note for her—why bother? It sounded like she thought I was a disgusting letch. Didn't she know I loved her more than any woman on the planet? Hadn't we been through enough together for her to know that I was hers forever? Apparently not. Locking the door behind me, I looked down the street to see if I could spot her car. I made a deal with God: if I saw it in the next sixty seconds, I would know she wanted to work it out and I would stay. I tossed my bag in the truck and waited. When she didn't come, I sighed, pulled out of the driveway and drove to the marina. I'd stay on the Happy Go Lucky tonight and figure out what my next move was. It would be cold as heck on the water this time of year, but it would have to do. I stopped by the grocery store to grab a few things for supper. I was starving. And to think I had planned on giving Carrie Jo an anniversary gift that she would never forget. I shook my head, did my shopping and headed to the boat.

About an hour later, I was sitting on the deck chewing an overcooked hamburger and watching the moonlight splash on the water. This was not the way I had planned to spend my anniversary. Wiping my hands with a napkin, I checked my phone yet again for a text or voicemail from Carrie Jo. Nothing. Not a peep. I stared off into the distance, sipping my beer and wondering what I could do to fix our current situation. We'd been through too much, seen too much to give up now, but this wouldn't work if only one of us was committed to seeing it through.

To make matters worse, I was seeing ghosts again. Not family ghosts this time, thankfully. Most were strangers, faded people who glared at me from curtained windows and sailed past me at inopportune moments. Even at home. Having other people around seemed to keep them away, though. Thank goodness for Doreen. When Carrie Jo wasn't there, Doreen was. The more living souls in the house, the merrier. People told me my "sight" was a gift, but I wouldn't call it that. I'd hated psychics and mediums when I was growing up, and now I'd become the thing I hated. Yeah, seeing ghosts was never fun. It always surprised me, and unlike on those stupid television shows, they never wanted anything or asked for anything. They didn't speak to me or ask for my help "finding the light." They were always unhappy or fixated on something. And likewise I never spoke to them or tried to communicate with them. Maybe I was going crazy like my mother.

To keep my mind straight, I decided to keep a diary. I wrote down what I saw, where I spotted the ghosts and the dates I saw them and for how long. I noticed that my ability to see ghosts was heightened during the full moon. What was I? Some sort of psychic werewolf? The only place I really found peace was on the water. I never saw anything out here. Once I thought I did, but it turned out to be nothing. And nobody had ever died on my boat—I'd bought it brand new just to be sure. Thank God for that.

Now I really thought I was going crazy. I saw a ghost yesterday, but it wasn't a true ghost—it was Detra Ann, who I knew for a fact was alive and well. What made it stranger was the ghost appeared in my home, on the stairs where she had been shot—probably by another ghost. I had called out to her, but she disappeared, shimmering for a second and then fluttering away like the end of an old movie reel. Her appearance had surprised me so much that I yelled. Doreen had stepped into the hallway to check on me. She swore that there was no one else in the house. I couldn't understand it. Maybe tomorrow I would go by the shop and see Detra Ann and Henri. I missed my friends. I missed my wife. How on earth had my life gone completely nuts?

I checked my phone one more time before I took it below to plug it in. I cleaned up the galley and headed to the shower. Carrie Jo wasn't going to call me. My wife was a stubborn woman but normally not this unreasonable. Why not just call it a night? After my shower, I fell asleep reading a book on mastering extrasensory perception. I woke with a stiff neck to the sound of someone calling my name.

"Ashland! You there?"

"Carrie Jo?" I tossed the book to the side and walked out on the deck. Libby Stevenson, a former schoolmate and my new attorney, stood on the dock with two cups of coffee. Her long dark hair shone in the sunlight. I had never seen her in casual clothing before, but today she wore blue jeans with a purposeful hole in the knee and a comfortable-looking blue t-shirt that read *LA: City of Dreams*. "May I come aboard? I come bearing gifts."

"Sure," I said, running my hands through my wild hair. My eyes felt sticky and my brain was tired—I must have stayed out later than I thought. "How did you know I was here? Did you talk to Carrie Jo?"

"I just happened to be riding by and saw your truck here. I know it's not a workday, but I figured I'd come take a peek at the infamous Happy Go Lucky." She handed me a cup of coffee.

I took it from her with a smile. "Infamous? I wouldn't say that."

"Well, it's the talk of the office. Roger Bosarge says that this is the boat you caught that prize-winning fish in— he thinks either this boat is lucky or you cheated. That was at the Deep Sea Fishing Rodeo a few years ago, right?" I nodded. "Someday you'll have to take me fishing." Pretty white teeth gleamed at me, and I couldn't help but smile back.

"You like to fish?"

"Big time. Growing up that's all we did. My dad believed in teaching us how to fish. I have to admit it's been a while since I've tossed a hook in the water, but I think I remember how to catch one." We sipped our coffees and sat in silence for a few minutes. "How did Mrs. Stuart like her gift?"

"I haven't given it to her yet."

"Oh, I see." Libby's blue eyes widened, and she clamped her lips for a second. "Sorry to hear that."

"It's no big deal."

"For what it's worth, I'd love to get a gift like that. Any woman would. I hope she knows how lucky she is."

"Truth be told, I'm the lucky one." I meant every word. I did love Carrie Jo. Despite this minor glitch, we'd gotten on very well considering the supernatural forces that continually arrayed themselves against us. She had helped me unravel my family's sordid past and set us free from a variety of self-inflicted curses. I was indeed a lucky man.

"That's sweet. You're just too good to be true."

I decided to change the subject. "So how is Jeremy? I heard he started his own veterinary clinic in Clarke County. Has he gotten over Kelly yet?"

Libby pursed her lips and rolled her eyes. "You know how my brother is. He's been in love with Kelly about as long as I've loved—" She stopped short, and I thought I saw a blush rise on her face. Taking another sip of her coffee, she continued, "Well, it's been a long time. At least she didn't leave him standing at the altar. He's got his animals so I think he'll be okay."

"He's got a terrific little sister—I'm sure he'll be fine."

She laughed dryly at the idea. "Relationship advice is truly not my field of expertise. If you need to evict a deadbeat, then I'm your girl. But I'm sure you're right. My brother is kind, handsome and successful—like you. He won't be lonely for long. Frankly, I would like to see him play the field a little more. Get out there and mingle. I think his biggest problem is he doesn't know what he's been missing."

I smiled at the idea of Jeremy mingling. He had been an excellent receiver, the best football player on our team; the guy was fearless on the field, but when it came to women he could hardly put two sentences together, at least before he met Kelly. I was bummed that the two of them had split up, but that kind of stuff happened.

"Which brings me to my next question…what made you get into an all-fired rush to get married? I thought you would be single forever."

"What makes you say that? I have never been a player."

Libby took a seat beside me and carefully removed the plastic lid from her steaming drink. "Oh, come on. It's me you're talking to. The unofficial little sister to the entire Bulldogs football team—I know the truth, Ash.

Let's see, there was Shay Dawson, Aimee Wilkinson, Jenna Daughtry…"

"Shay and I are just friends, always have been. Aimee…I did like her, but she moved senior year. And Jenna wasn't the kind of girl to stay with one guy for too long."

"You know, Jenna's changed a lot. Can you believe she married Tony Merritt? Better her than me. I don't think I could ever be a preacher's wife. And then there was Detra Ann. I always thought if I didn't marry you, she'd be the one to put a ring on your finger. Y'all were inseparable."

My phone rang, and I unplugged it from the charger. "This is Ashland."

"Morning, sunshine! Is Carrie Jo coming in today? I told her I'd be here this morning, but she hasn't showed up. If she's going to be late could you ask her to bring some breakfast when she comes in? I'm starving." Rachel Kowalski always talked like that. She threw whole paragraphs at you without taking a breath. Young, ambitious, and completely loyal. I felt guilty that I didn't know what to tell her.

"I'm not at the house right now, so I'm not sure."

"Did she mention coming in? Because that was the plan yesterday. Here I thought I was late. You two must have stayed up too late last night. Oh, the married life."

"Actually, I stayed on the boat last night."

She was silent for a moment. "Sorry, Mr. Stuart. Didn't mean to be nosy. Well, I'll call the house phone again. She's not answering her cell, and her car is here."

"Her car is there? Tell you what—I'll head that way and bring you both some breakfast."

"Sounds yummy. Thanks so much! Bye!"

I dialed Carrie Jo's number, but she still wasn't answering. Her cheery voice asked me to leave a voicemail. I hung up and tried the house phone. Still no dice. Doreen didn't work on Sundays, so I'd have to go check myself. That familiar nagging feeling that something was wrong began to grow in my gut.

"Thanks for the coffee, Libby, but I have to go."

"I overheard the conversation. I hope everything is all right with Carrie Jo. Need me to tag along?"

"No, I'm sure it's nothing. My wife hasn't been feeling well lately."

"I'm just a phone call away if you need me."

"Thanks." I began collecting my things and practically ran down the pier to my car. What a jerk I'd been! I should have stayed home last night instead of pouting on the boat. I haphazardly dialed her phone again as I peeled out of the parking lot slinging rocks and dust. The harbormaster yelled at me, but I didn't have time to explain.

No answer. This isn't good.

Adjusting my rearview mirror as I sped down the causeway, I nearly screamed. For a second it appeared that someone was in my backseat. I saw a face—a man's face. He had pale skin, dark hair that curled around the collar of his crumbling white shirt and empty eyes. I could barely form a thought before he vanished in a less than a second. My car swerved erratically until I got it under control. I swore under my breath as I tried to slow my breathing.

No. This isn't good at all.

Chapter Six—Delilah

I ran as fast as my feet would carry me away from Adam's shop. He shouted my name again, but I didn't stop to answer him. I didn't know where I planned to go—back to Maundy's, I supposed. Where else could I go? Anywhere but with Adam. In my mind I could still see his sweaty back writhing over Blessing Harper, the leatherman's middle daughter. She'd been panting beneath him, repeating his name hungrily, when I walked into the store room of the carpentry shop. I wouldn't have even walked in if he'd bothered to close the door. It was almost as if he wanted to get caught.

Adam came running after me, still shirtless. "Stop, Delilah!" He reached toward me and grabbed my shoulder, spinning me around forcefully.

"Get your damn hands off me!" I shouted at him.

"So now you are swearing? What else has Maundy Weaver taught you?"

"Me? You have no room to criticize me, Adam Iverson! How could you do this?"

Suddenly he stiffened, his chin raised defiantly, and peered down at me with icy blue eyes. "This is your fault," he said viciously as he pointed a finger at me. "You are the one who decided we should no longer be together. Remember the speech you gave me, *sister*? You are the one who wanted to forget about us, and for what? To claim an old name and a fortune you will never have. What would our parents think about you now, Delilah?"

I slapped him as hard as I could right across the face. My hand stung, and his pale skin instantly turned red with the vivid prints from my fingers and palm. He took a step toward me but then froze, his glance riveted to some action over my shoulder. I turned myself, relieved to see Jackson Keene walking toward us, his face dark with concern.

"Here comes your new lover to save you, sister. Now I see why you pushed me out of your bed." I gasped at his insinuation, feeling now as if I had been the one slapped, especially in light of the fact Adam was walking away with bits of straw on his naked back. He didn't wait around to hear my reply, not that I would have given him one. In his mind he would always be right, no matter how wrong he was. He was a fool. His tall, lumbering frame headed back to the carpentry shop.

Some women would have fallen apart; I knew a few who would do just that having worked in Maundy's shop and in her private parlor for the past few months. The stories I'd heard I would never have imagined. Maundy was right—women did talk too much, about too many things and especially about one another. Unfortunately as of yet, I had heard nothing about Claudette Page. But I had heard plenty of tales of adultery, babies born out of wedlock, husbands who asked their wives for strange acts in the bedroom, and it was all proof of what I suspected. Marriage was not so much a thing to be desired as a hardship that crushed the soul—at least the female soul. The more I heard, the less I wanted to be Mrs. Anyone. How could I have ever imagined that I would be Adam's wife?

Instead of weeping like a child, I relished the rebellion that rose up within me. Adam had been the one who wanted to return to Mobile, and I had agreed. He was the one who wanted to come back "home" and make a name for himself, and I had come with him. We had done everything he wanted and nothing else. I refused to live my life according to his whims anymore. I vowed to never be under the control of any man ever again. And I would never surrender my right to my family name and my inheritance. I was going to have everything I wanted in this life—even if that meant living without love! All the passion, all the love I had believed I felt for Adam had been nothing but an illusion.

"Miss Page, may I be of assistance?" Mr. Keene glared toward Adam's shop, obviously ready to defend my honor. If only he knew that I didn't have any honor left. But I did not worry that Adam would tell him. He would rather die than have the world know he had been romantically involved with his "sister." Why? Half the town knew the truth—I was the bastard child of Christine Cottonwood and Hoyt Page. The other half believed everything Claudette Page and her unofficial "morality society" told them. That I was a nobody, an incestuous scam artist bent on destroying the Page family name and with that the City of Mobile. Last week the woman had the nerve to send me a check for five thousand dollars and a one-way train ticket out of town. I ripped up the check and sent it back with a little note of my own.

Keep your money, Aunt Claudette. In the future, please send all correspondence to my attorney, Jackson Keene.

"Yes, Mr. Keene, I believe you can be of help to me. I would like to find a new place to live. I think it's time I moved out of the store. In fact, I would like to sell the whole building." He blinked, his intelligent eyes full of surprise.

"Mr. Iverson may have something to say about that."

"I have full confidence in your negotiation talents. If Adam does cause a fuss, let him know that I am willing to relinquish all the other Iverson properties to him…and remind him that he has as much to lose as I do when it comes to reputation. All I want are the proceeds from this building. I am sure that is what my parents would have wanted."

"I'll make the arrangements, Miss Page, and begin inquiries on a new home. I think we can find something for you…here in town, correct?"

"Yes," I said with a smile, pretending that he didn't look relieved. "I intend to keep working with Maundy Weaver. Maybe something on Florence Street or perhaps Carlen? Is the Winslow home still available? The yellow one with the wisteria out front?" He smiled and nodded. Together we walked back to my shop, side by side on the dusty wooden walkway. I glanced back once to make sure Adam wasn't glaring at us, but I needn't have worried. He didn't show his face again. He wouldn't with Mr. Keene around. Seeing the street now crowded, I decided to take the back way around.

"You know, if you sell the shop, Claudette Page will think she's won."

"Let her think that. What it really means is—what's that poker term? Oh yes, 'I'm all in.'"

He laughed. "I never figured you for a poker player."

"It's a recent hobby I've taken up, and I am told I'm quite good at it."

"I believe that completely," he replied, smiling down at me. "So a small home, like a cottage?"

"Yes, nothing too pricy."

"You know, according to Dr. Page's will, you technically own a few properties near here."

"Yes, and if I step foot near one, his sister will have me tossed out before I unpack the first trunk. No, I don't think I'm ready to go to war. Not yet, Mr. Keene."

"I like your spirit, Miss Page." By his smile, I could tell he meant it. Still, I refused to blush like a teenage virgin. "It is nearly suppertime. Will you do me the honor of having supper with me this evening? We could talk more about what it is you're looking for, in the way of houses. Did I tell you that the judge who will be hearing your case came in on the train today? I have already taken the liberty of introducing myself to him. I think the high-and-mighty Claudette Page may find this new judge less flexible on the law."

"Flexible. That's a nice word for it," I huffed, ignoring his question. "Judge Parker barely even heard our case before he ruled against me." A few people walked down the side street and stared at us, but I had trained myself not to look at their faces. I didn't even mind that some women saw me and crossed to the other side of the street, as if being illegitimate were a disease to be caught. Mr. Keene didn't seem to mind at all.

"You were right to appeal, and you *will* win. Of that I am sure. The morality law that Judge Parker cited is a relic—almost as much of a relic as the judge himself. I feel sure that by this summer you'll be sipping lemonade on the porch of some Page property." He smiled again—it was a nice thing to see.

Jackson Keene was not overtly handsome, not like Adam with his chiseled, Nordic features, impressive height and fit physique. From working in Maundy's shop I could take Mr. Keene's measure without ever putting a tape to him. Barely 5'10", he had a sturdy medium build with flashing blue eyes and a manicured mustache that hinted at pink lips. I knew for a fact that the ladies enjoyed looking at him because anytime he visited the shop there was a wave of excited chatter after he left and sometimes even while he was there. He was five years my senior but had a young face, and I believed if he ever shaved he'd probably look much younger than he was.

He paused at the back door of my shop as I pulled the key from my purse. I thanked him for walking me home, but he didn't leave right away. He stood with his hat in his hand, waiting for my answer to his invitation.

With a polite smile I answered, "Yes, I will have supper with you. Step inside, Mr. Keene. You can make yourself comfortable in the shop. There are some chairs behind the counter. I would like to tidy up if you don't mind. I won't be a minute."

"Certainly, I will be happy to wait." He followed me into the shop, and I walked up the stairs sure that he was watching me. I changed my clothes quickly. Although Adam no longer lived in the apartment with me—he'd moved into the quarter house attached to the shop—it wasn't beyond him to come stomping up the stairs without warning. Tidying myself as quickly as I could, I scowled at myself in the mirror. Hadn't I just sworn off men? Here I was, going to dinner with my attorney. Tongues would wag, but weren't they already? Again rebellion filled my heart.

What did these people know about me?

I dipped my fingers in the water basin and smoothed my hair in an attempt to tidy up the curls that sprang up around my face. I had a new gray dress with a thin black ribbon that ran across the top of the bodice. It had a modest neckline with three-quarter sleeves, a bit old fashioned perhaps but perfectly respectable for a business dinner.

In a few minutes I was ready, but I lingered at the mirror. I was still young and some called me pretty, although it had been a long time since anyone had complimented me on my appearance.

Like I had so many times since I first read that letter from Dr. Page, I studied my face in the mirror. I wondered whose eyes those were, whose nose? Did my mother have a pretty voice? How did she die? I would never know, but at least I had life. I supposed I should be grateful that I wasn't abandoned at an orphanage or drowned in a river. With a frown I reached for my perfume and sprayed my hair once before I rejoined my guest.

I heard Mr. Keene sliding the wooden chair back; it made a hash sound, and I tried not to stare at the scrape on the floor. He walked toward the back door but I stopped him.

"No, not the back door. Let's go this way, if you don't mind." I waved him to the front. I took the key out of my black satin purse and opened the front door.

"As you wish." He followed me out and waited patiently as I fumbled with the key. My black lace glove caught the metal, but I quickly unsnagged myself and locked the door. "You look lovely," he whispered.

"Thank you, Mr. Keene. Where are we dining tonight?"

"Let's take my carriage. Have you been to Patterson's yet?"

"No, I haven't, but I am quite hungry." I climbed aboard the carriage and arranged my dress neatly. Mr. Keene sat beside me, and together we rode through town with our heads held high. As we traveled, he told me stories about the war, how various businesses and families had fared and what he thought about the prospects for the city. He had been born in Mississippi but had been in Mobile since the end of the war. I did not think it polite to tell him I probably knew more than he did about Mobile society, as I was Maundy's friend and was privy to much information. So I listened and nodded appropriately.

We drove at least twenty minutes, passing the cathedral and the expansive oak groves that lined Dauphin Street. I had not been this far down Dauphin since I was a child, and I could barely remember those times anymore. The carriage turned down an unmarked road, and I suddenly felt a bit panicked. Where were we going? The carriage paused in front of a looming plantation at the end of a wide red dirt lane. As we drew closer, I could see that the house wasn't completely empty; a few lamps shone through the windows, and gas lamps flickered along the carriageway. Despite the light it didn't feel like a happy place, not in the least. I shivered and pulled my wrap closer. "Is this Patterson's? I didn't know we were going to someone's home."

"You've never been here, Miss Page? This is Seven Sisters."

I caught my breath. "My mother's home?"

"Yes. She moved here from north Alabama when she married Jeremiah Cottonwood. Truth be told, it was her money that kept this house in the Cottonwood name. It's no secret that her husband could not manage his pocketbook, much less an estate of this size."

In a determined voice I said, "I want to go inside."

"I don't know if that's such a good idea. I had no intention of stopping—I merely wanted you to see the place. I don't think anyone lives there anymore, except for a few of the former slaves and occasionally some obscure relative. And...not to cast aspersions, Miss Page, but the current resident is probably a

Cottonwood and thus is less likely to make you welcome. No offense, of course."

"I want to go inside," I said again as I slid clumsily out of the carriage seat. The red clay dirt crumbled into powder beneath my feet, evidence of the long dry spell Mobile had endured recently. Mr. Keene stepped down beside me and offered me his arm.

"Let us go and make our acquaintance." I slid my arm through his and held my breath as the massive front door opened. A tall black man stepped out on the porch. Other faces peered at us from the hallway. My grip on Mr. Keene's arm tightened as we walked up the steps.

The attorney called to the man in a friendly voice, "Good evening. We would like to call on the lady or gentleman of the house. I am Jackson Keene, and this is Miss Delilah...Iverson."

"Delilah Page," I corrected him. I wasn't going to hide my identity like some criminal. He squeezed my hand gently. The tall man showed no emotion one way or another. His dark eyes revealed nothing.

"Please come in, sir, ma'am. My name is Stokes. I will tell Miss Cottonwood you are here. I think she's been expecting you." With a puzzled look, Mr. Keene followed the man into the house and I trailed behind him. Pulling my gray silk wrap even tighter around my shoulders, I nearly fainted at the sight.

The house was easily the biggest home I had ever visited. Maundy Weaver's was nothing in comparison to this place, and I thought her home grand. That was before I set foot in Seven Sisters. Under my feet was a colorful rug with big blue flowers. It looked worn and frayed at the edges, but the floors were neatly kept. A side table held a vase full of dying flowers, the shriveled petals the only flaw in the scene. The place smelled like soap and magnolias. Stokes had walked up the wooden staircase, leaving us to wait in the foyer.

I saw a small fire burning in the room to my left, and like a moth to a flame I walked toward it. Mr. Keene did not follow me, and I did not seek his permission to go. I still couldn't believe I was here—at Seven Sisters. *This may be the closest I'll ever be to my mother!*

So many fine things, and yet an overwhelming sadness pervaded the room. It almost made me cry. A small collection of books lay on a round cherrywood table near the fireplace. I couldn't help but touch them. I thought Miss Cottonwood must like to read, a hobby that I had not taken up faithfully. I read quite well but found that reading for long periods of time made me sleepy. After glancing at the books for a few minutes, I warmed my hands at the fire.

I heard voices in the foyer but didn't turn to look. I stepped back from the fire and saw a large portrait hanging on the wall. I couldn't imagine why I hadn't noticed it when I first came in. The frame was painted gold, and I could see the artist's signature in the corner: *R. Ball.*

It was a portrait of a young woman dressed in a beautiful coral gown. Her shiny brown hair was arranged in a complicated yet flattering hairstyle, and dainty earbobs dangled from her pretty ears. She had a faraway look in her eyes, and on her lips was a hint of a smile. I wondered who she might be. My mother? Some relative I would never know or be able to claim? As if someone were reading my mind, a voice beside me answered my question.

"That is Calpurnia Cottonwood—the daughter of the late Jeremiah and Christine Cottonwood. From what I understand she was the beauty of the county. She disappeared some time ago, before I was born."

I wanted to continue to stare at the portrait, especially now that I knew the woman's identity. To think this was my sister Calpurnia, and not just a half-sister or a stepsister but my true blood sister, if Dr. Page's account was to be believed. She was riveting. Still, I couldn't be rude to my hostess; I had not been invited into this room. The least I could do was be polite.

Pulling my attention from the portrait, I faced the new lady of the house. Younger than me and not as tall, her voice didn't quite match her face. Although she was young, she had a deep voice and intelligent hazel eyes. I could tell she didn't give two figs about her appearance: her clothes were smart but not too stylish, and she wore her dark blond hair in a simple bun. My hostess did not extend her hand or offer a smile. I could sense that she was suspicious, but who could blame her with two strangers showing up at her mansion uninvited? If she did know who I was, then she must think I was crazy or an upstart. Honestly, I didn't know why I had wanted to come inside. Visiting Seven Sisters had not been on my list of things to do. The idea had never crossed my mind before we arrived there this evening.

My attorney cleared his throat and offered an explanation. "Please pardon the intrusion, madam. We were just passing by, and the house is such a lovely Mobile landmark that we could not resist visiting it. Let me introduce myself properly. I am Jackson Keene and this is my friend, Delilah Iverson-Page." I thought I saw her eyes widen a little, but Miss Cottonwood did not comment or ask questions. In fact, she ignored Mr. Keene entirely.

"Yes," she said as she stepped toward me, "you have the look of her. I have seen you before—at Miss Weaver's fitting parlor. Now I remember. But you don't remember me? My name is Karah Cottonwood."

Embarrassed at the slight I stammered, "We see many women on a daily basis. Forgive me if I don't. Did I work on your dress?"

She smiled, and I was reminded of that phrase, 'the cat that ate the canary'. I had a feeling I was the canary. "No, you didn't work on my dress. I came to place an order with Miss Weaver. We have not been introduced, not officially." She turned her attention to the portrait. "Is this why you are here? To assess some claim on Seven Sisters?" She finally spoke to Mr. Keene. "You are an attorney, correct?"

With a courteous wave of his hand, he shook his head. "As Miss Page's attorney, I can assure you that my client has not expressed any desire to make a claim on Seven Sisters. She was merely curious to see the place, and I must confess she had no idea I was bringing her here. Please accept my apology. It was not my intention to inconvenience you." Miss Cottonwood listened, but her gaze didn't leave my face. I felt compelled to speak.

"I have no such desire."

The young lady must have been satisfied with that answer, for she took a deep breath and a sincere smile crossed her face. "Have you had any supper? I was about to take mine, and there is more than enough. Would you two be my guests? I never knew your sister, Miss Page, or the late Mrs. Cottonwood, but I will be happy to answer any of your questions if I can."

Now it was my turn to smile. "Oh, yes. Thank you very much."

"Follow me." Miss Cottonwood walked with her hands in front of her. Wherever she was from, she was certainly trained to behave like a lady. An evil thought crossed my mind. What if I did claim the house? Shouldn't it be partly mine? Miss Cottonwood was living in grand style in this grand house, enjoying my mother's wealth while I was laboring in the dress shop. Then I instantly felt guilty. My current situation was not Miss Cottonwood's responsibility or anyone else's. She had not wronged me.

We walked down the broad hallway, and I tried not to stare at the oil paintings that filled the walls. We walked to the door and stepped into the most beautiful room I had ever seen. With some pride Miss Cottonwood said, "This is the Blue Room—it is my favorite room in the house. The servants tell me it was once a place for musical concerts and spiritual readings. I think it's a delightful space." For the first time I heard youthful excitement in her voice. "Please make yourself welcome while I go tell Docie to set two more plates." With a polite nod she left us, closing the door behind her.

"Mr. Keene, have you ever seen anything like this place?" I explored the room, curious to examine every nook and cranny. On one wall a built-in shelf displayed a collection of ceramic puppies. I longed to pick them up and hold each one in my hand. I imagined they felt cool and smooth, but I did not dare. My hostess would not appreciate strangers destroying her property.

"I can't say that I have. I have been in some grand old homes, but I have to admit this is the grandest. I hope you hold no grudge toward me because I brought you here without warning. On reflection perhaps this was not a good idea. Perhaps it is wrong to show you all this knowing that you could never claim it."

"I am grateful that you did. I would never have had the courage to come here myself. I suppose I could press the issue if I wanted to, but I am happy with what I have—or will have." Tapping the spines of a collection of books by some obscure author I added, "It's never been about the money, Mr. Keene. I hope you know that. I want my name. My real name. I want to hold my head up high and introduce myself as Delilah Page. It is what my father wanted, or else he would never have written to me."

"Yes, the letter." His voice dropped. "Let us keep that letter to ourselves, if at all possible."

"Why? I'm not ashamed. I am who I am. I'm not less of a person despite my unhappy situation."

"No insult to you, Miss Page, but let me remind you that your father confessed to murder in that letter. In fact, I suspect that he did indeed murder Miss Cottonwood's father."

My face paled at the reminder. "I haven't forgotten that, Mr. Keene."

"Please call me Jackson."

Before I could argue with him, I heard yelling in the hall. Curious to discover the source of the disturbance, I walked to the door and opened it slightly. The young Miss Cottonwood was arguing with an older woman—a woman I had never seen before. "Just stop it! Do what I ask!" The older woman raised her head and stared at me. Miss Cottonwood spun about and saw me standing there. With a swish of her skirts she left the old woman in the hallway and came toward me, her face a mask of determination.

"Come, Miss Page. Let's sit together. Dinner will be here soon." Leading us to a round table in the corner of the room, she sat as if she were a queen at court. She had a natural elegance, an elegance I admired but did not have. As she and Mr. Keene exchanged pleasantries and talked about Mobile, I stared around the room, silently comparing myself to Miss Cottonwood. I was taller by at least a foot, and my dark hair was prone to curl, while hers was smooth and not as dark. Could it be true that we were related somehow? I wondered what Mr. Keene thought about her. I knew nothing about her, but I was dying to know where she was from and who she was related to. As if she read my mind,

Miss Cottonwood said, "I suppose you are both wondering about me."

"We do seem to be at a disadvantage. Excuse me for asking, but is that an English accent I detect?"

"Yes, Mr. Keene. I spent quite a bit of time abroad with my mother before coming to Mobile."

I finally asked the question I had been dying to ask, "Who is your mother, Miss Cottonwood?"

With an even, steely gaze she answered me, "My mother is Isla Beaumont, daughter of Olivia Beaumont, sister of Christine Cottonwood."

"Are we related then in some way?" I asked her, my voice shakier than I expected.

"I think we are cousins, Miss Page."

"And your father?" I asked, ignoring Mr. Keene's scowl. It wasn't the proper thing to ask, but people asked me all the time, didn't they?

"Jeremiah Cottonwood. Unfortunately I never knew him." We three sat in silence for a full minute before she spoke again. "It seems there are a great many secrets here in this house. Don't you agree, Miss Page?"

"Yes, I do." A flurry of questions filled my brain. What happened to my mother, to my sister? What did my mother look like? Did she leave me anything? A note or a letter? But it was too soon in our acquaintance to bombard Miss Cottonwood with those queries. I had already broken protocol with my rude question once, but I had to know for sure. The servant, the older angry one with the slick dark hair, came in with platters of food and plunked them down unceremoniously on the linen-covered table.

"Thank you, Docie. Now please bring the wine for our guests."

She glared at Miss Cottonwood, who tried to ignore her. Our hostess placed her linen napkin in her lap, and I did the same. With a shiny gold fork she pierced a piece of ham and placed it on her plate. I helped myself to a piece of warm bread and a pat of butter. It was a simple but delicious meal. As she cut her meat into tiny pieces, she asked, "What are your plans, Miss Page? Do you intend to stay in Mobile?"

"I do indeed. This is my home. Granted, I have legal battles ahead of me, but I don't plan to turn tail and run. Mr. Keene is helping me adjudicate my case with the court. I am sure you have heard all about it."

"Where would I have heard anything like that? Do you think me a gossip?"

Her question surprised me. "I didn't mean to imply that," I said defensively.

Docie returned with a glass pitcher full of burgundy wine. She poured the young woman's drink and set the pitcher on the table. She didn't offer to pour ours or wait to be dismissed but glared at me again before leaving us alone. Aware of her servant's rudeness, Miss Cottonwood's cheeks reddened. She stood and poured our drinks, and then returned to her seat. Mr. Keene kept silent, watching the two of us. I thought I spotted a hint of a smile on his lips.

"I think what Miss Page means is that she is aware her situation is the source of quite a bit of gossip amongst certain quarters of Mobile society. It would not surprise either of us if you had heard something negative about her. However, having enjoyed her acquaintance these past months, I can vouch that she is a kind lady with a good many fine qualities." He sipped his wine and said seriously, "You know, it might be beneficial to you both to form some kind of alliance. Even an unofficial one. After all, you are family and face similar situations."

Ignoring the last part of his statement, she asked, "What sort of alliance?"

"Because of your unique social positions, it might be wise to make a united front against anyone who would deny either of you your heritage. At least you could stand up for one another, if the situation called for it." I watched the candles on the table flicker as I sipped my wine. My lips felt dry, and my heart pounded.

"I agree—if you are so inclined, Miss Page." She set down her fork and knife and watched me.

"Very well, I agree. Do you have an attorney, Miss Cottonwood?"

"Karah, please. If we are to form an alliance, then we should call each other by our given names, I think. And no, not yet."

"Please call me Delilah. And if you don't think it out of place, I would like to recommend Mr. Keene. He's been a great help to me. I am sure he could help you too."

She smiled broadly. "Would you be willing to take me on, Mr. Keene? I have had no luck with finding adequate counsel. At first lawyers were calling on me nearly every day to offer their services, and now I can't seem to find any help. I confess I feel somewhat desperate. If it weren't for my mother's nest egg, I would have nothing at all. While she's away, all I can do is wait—it's most frustrating."

I knew exactly what had happened—Claudette Page. The woman held a lot of influence here. There was no doubt she was using that influence to force us both to leave Mobile.

Mr. Keene nodded. "I would be happy to do some research for you. Let's meet again to talk about the particulars."

His answer pleased her. She raised her glass to me and said, "To new friends."

It must have been the wine, but I smiled and added, "To family."

When we left that evening, I felt happy, happier than I had in a long time. Karah and I had plans to meet the following week. I was to return to Seven Sisters for tea, and my cousin promised me that I would be given full access to my mother's belongings. I could hardly believe it. As the carriage rolled down the long driveway, I looked back just to prove to myself that I wasn't dreaming.

I saw the curtains move in an upstairs room of the house. A dark face peered down at me. It was an old woman, much older than the angry Docie. Even from this distance, I could see her expression clearly: she was afraid. She shook her head and mouthed some words, but I couldn't understand them. I felt troubled and turned to ask Mr. Keene to stop and turn around, but when I looked back the woman was gone. I pulled my wrap closer.

I didn't look back again.

Chapter Seven—Carrie Jo

I woke up to a rough tongue licking my face. A friendly cat meowed at me before he stalked off. At least he was friendlier than the furry bag of claws that had assailed me in the cemetery. I sat up, wondering where I was. Cold, stone floor, wooden pews, high vaulted ceilings— I was in a church. I stood and dusted off my clothing. Morning light filtered through the stained glass windows. Under normal circumstances I would've found the imagery beautiful, but these were not normal circumstances. I picked up my purse from the ground and looked around to make sure I hadn't lost anything. Checking my hands and legs, I didn't see any injuries, but the side of my face stung. I touched a ragged scratch on my cheek, probably delivered by the evil cat.

Have I really been here all night? How did I get here? And where is here?

I heard the sound of a key ring jostling; the metal security gate screeched and then the side door of the church swung open. The emerging air felt fresh and warm, and I was thankful for the sunshine. I didn't know whether to call out or to hide. My indecisiveness had me frozen to the spot.

"Well, good morning. Have you been here all night? Get a bit of prayer in?" an older gentleman in a black suit called to me as he shoved the keys in his pocket. His head was semi-bald; white wisps of hair poked out from his temples, and the morning light surrounded him like a halo.

"I'm not sure," I confessed. "I must have fallen asleep. If you'll excuse me." Great. Now I was lying to a priest. In a church, no less.

"No need to rush off. Is this your first time visiting the basilica?" The more he spoke, the more I discerned a heavy French accent. Odd to find a French priest in Mobile, wasn't it?

"Um, basilica?"

"Yes, young lady. You are at the Cathedral Basilica of the Immaculate Conception. I am Father Portier." After a moment he asked, "Are you sure you are all right?"

"Yes, I am. I just…I'd better go. Thank you, Father."

"Very well, thank you for visiting. I must go ring the bells. Can't be late."

"Yes, of course." I strolled toward the open door. The downtown streets were becoming busy now with morning traffic. Then I thought if anyone could answer my questions about the supernatural, surely it would be a priest, right? I glanced at my watch. It was nearly eight o'clock, just two minutes till. "Father if you don't mind, I do have a question."

He smiled pleasantly. "And I will be happy to answer it after I ring the bells. I shall return in a moment."

I sat in a back pew and waited as he began to climb the narrow stairs that led to the belfry. In just a minute the bells began to chime, sure to wake up any nearby residents who were still asleep. It was a beautiful sound. The old man returned to the sanctuary and walked toward me. "Ah, still here. I was hoping you would not change your mind. Not everyone likes the sound of bells, you know."

"I think they're lovely."

"That's nice. Now what is your question, my dear?" He sat in the pew across the aisle from me, resting his gnarled hands on the back of the wooden seat in front of him.

"It's probably going to sound strange, especially coming from someone you don't know, and…I must confess I am not a Catholic."

"We are all children of God. What do you want to know?"

"Thank you for saying that. I am not sure God knows who I am, but it's nice of you to say so."

"I have a feeling He knows all about you, young lady."

"Do you believe in the supernatural, Father? I mean, the world of ghosts and supernatural activity. Is it all evil? Maybe figments of our imagination?"

He considered my question for a moment, then pointed at a nearby statue. It was the Virgin Mary holding the baby Jesus. The statue was painted in bright colors, and on her breast was painted a purple heart. "Do you see that statue?" I nodded. "Do you see the rose she's stepping on?"

"Yes, I do."

"Whenever you see a rose in a painting or statue of the Blessed Virgin, you should look for the secret."

"Secret? I don't understand."

"Look carefully at her hands. Do you see anything unusual?"

I got up from my seat and walked toward the statue. I studied Mary's hands for a moment, then caught my breath. "She's holding something in her hand…it looks like a pearl! What does that mean?"

"That is the question." He rose from the pew, walked toward the statue and studied it with me. He stood looking up at the artwork and then smiled at me. "Not even church scholars can agree on the reason for that pearl. Some say it's a symbol of the purity of the Virgin, while others say it represents the Parable of the Pearl, and there are other more fantastic opinions with which I won't bore you."

"That's interesting, but I'm not sure what that has to do with…"

He chuckled. "Ah, to be young again. So impatient to know all the answers. That is my point. The truth about the pearl's meaning is a mystery. It is there, we can see it, we know it is an unusual thing and this statue is very old. Much older than even me, and that is quite old." He smiled pleasantly. "But we don't know what it means. You see, the world is full of mysteries, not the least of which is the subject of the supernatural. Like this pearl, it is something to be discovered and defined by each man, each woman."

I stared at the pearl and considered his words. He asked kindly, "Does that help you at all, or have I confused you more?"

"Yes, it does help." I did feel more peaceful. He didn't answer my question, not directly, but perhaps he was right. This was a subject that had no answer, no black-and-white definition. "I'd better go now. My husband will be looking for me."

"I am sure he will be. Take care, and mind those steps. I would hate for an expectant mother to trip on the cathedral stairs."

"How did you know?" My hand flew to my stomach protectively.

"When you get to be as old as I am, dear lady, it is easy to spot the glow on a young mother's face."

I smiled and touched my flushed cheek before I turned to walk out of the church. Such a nice old man. Almost made me wish I were Catholic. I walked down the steps and out to the courtyard. I was on Conception Street near the intersection with St. Anthony. Yes, I knew this church; I just never knew the name. I turned around to get a better view of the old building and caught my breath. The place had two huge towers flanking the massive sanctuary. Round domes sat atop the towers, which must have housed the church bells. To my surprise, the gate was locked again. I couldn't believe Father Portier had managed to close it so quickly and so quietly.

Curious now, I walked back to the church, but it was locked up tight. A red-haired gentleman wearing green coveralls walked toward me whistling. "Need to get in there? I was just about to open up. Sorry I'm late. Hey, you're new."

"Yes, I'm new, but I was just in there talking to Father Portier."

He pushed up his thick glasses. "What are you talking about?"

"I was just talking to your priest, Father Portier. Older man, balding, with white hair?"

He looked around as if someone might jump out at him. "Is this some kind of joke, lady?"

"No joke. I swear it's the truth. Just ask him yourself. He's right inside."

With a skeptical look, the man opened the gate and stepped inside. There was no one around.

"He rang the bells a few minutes ago. Are you going to tell me I made that up?"

"Those bells have been on a timer since the early '90s. Listen, I don't know what you're into, drugs, booze or whatever, but you need help, lady."

I backed away and walked out of the church. By the time I made it to the end of the sidewalk, I was already running. I didn't stop until I reached Conception Street. When I got home I wasn't shaking anymore. I was tired and hungry, and I had butterflies. Mostly, I was happy to have something else to think about besides Father Portier and the weird experience I'd just had.

I walked up the sidewalk, happy to see Ashland's truck in the driveway. What was I going to say to him, coming home in yesterday's clothes? *Sorry, babe, I passed out in a church.*

As if he could hear my thoughts, he bounded out of the house. "Thank God! Are you okay? Where have you been, Carrie Jo?" Before I could answer him, he put his arms around me and pulled me to his chest. "You had me so worried."

"I am sorry. I'm a jerk." I clung to him, feeling ashamed that I had not told him the news about our child. Now was as good a time as any. "I will explain everything, I promise, but first I have to tell you something. I can't go another minute without telling you. I should have already told you, but I was so angry. I know it was stupid. I'm so sorry."

"What is it?" His bright blue eyes searched mine, and he held my hands. "Are you sure you're okay?"

"Ashland Stuart, you are going to be a father."

He dropped my hands, and his eyes widened. "Are you serious?"

"Absolutely. But if you don't believe me, you can wait six and a half to seven months and see for yourself."

A big, beautiful smile crept across his face. He picked me up and kissed me passionately. Before I could say "Boo," he carried me into the house. His worries had clearly vanished.

"We'll need a bigger house. And furniture." He put me down and kissed me again.

"Okay, calm down. I've had a rough night. That was the good news. Now I have something else to tell you. It's about Delilah Iverson, and something else happened. I was at a church. Well, it was a gate and then a church. But Ash, I'm starving. I would love some of your cheese grits."

"I can take a hint. Why don't you call Rachel and tell her you're going to be late? She's been almost as worried about you as I have. Why is your car at the office?"

"It broke down. Brand-new BMW, and it won't start. Food first, Mr. Stuart. I'll go change if you don't mind." I touched his hand. "Are you sure you're happy? We've never actually talked about having kids."

"Of course I'm happy. Aren't you?"

"Yes, I am."

"Good. Then you go change, I'll cook, and we'll meet back here in ten minutes."

"Yes sir," I said playfully as I walked up the stairs.

Chapter Eight—Carrie Jo

At 9:45 p.m., I finally pressed the send button on the proposal, shooting it off to Desmond Taylor with a weary smile. I couldn't have done it without Ashland and Rachel. Even Chip helped out by picking up the takeout and pulling up old purchase orders from our Seven Sisters job. It was definitely a team effort, and that felt good. Hopefully we would hear something positive from Mr. Taylor soon. I leaned back in my chair and sighed. What a weird forty-eight hours this had been! I'd been so busy with finalizing the prelim proposal I hardly had time to mull over my supernatural encounter with the cemetery light and the friendly priest. When I retold the story to my husband over breakfast he didn't question my sanity.

Looking as tired as I did, Ashland began picking up our dinner remnants, empty takeout boxes and half-empty water bottles, while I closed up shop on the computer. With bleary eyes I closed the folders, remembering to save our work one last time. I was just about to shut the whole thing down when my inbox dinged. I hoped it was Mr. Taylor emailing me back to confirm that he received the file, but it wasn't my prospective client. The email was from Alice and Myron Reed.

"Uh-oh."

"What is it?"

"I just received an email from the Reeds. I wonder what this is about." I could tell from Ashland's raised eyebrows that he was as suspicious as I was. Nothing good ever came from chatting with the Reeds. Since their daughter's arrest they barely spoke to me, but I suppose I couldn't blame them. A few months after Mia's commitment in the state mental hospital, I got a notification from the Reeds' attorney of a pending civil action, but then they suddenly dropped it. I had no idea what they were thinking—then or now.

"Babe, why don't you wait until tomorrow to read that? I'm sure it's not anything super important."

I tapped my finger nervously on the mouse pad. "You are probably right, but if I don't check it I'm going to spend all night thinking about it. I mean, what if Mia somehow got free? Wouldn't you want to know if she might be lurking in the bushes?" I said with a sad smile.

Ashland sat up straight and tossed the leftovers in the garbage can. "If for some reason that ever happened I'd be on the phone to the governor." With a worried expression he added, "There's no way that woman should be let loose on the public. Here, I can bag this garbage up in a minute. Let's open the message now and see what is happening."

I waited for him to join me, and then I clicked on the email.

Dear Carrie Jo,

We are writing to tell you some sad news. We lost our daughter Mia this morning…

I gasped at what I was reading. This couldn't be true!

Services for Mia will be held Tuesday at Grant Funeral Home in Birmingham, Alabama. We thought it was only right that we invite you to speak on her behalf, as you were her closest friend. If you cannot attend her service we understand, but please know that you always hold a special place in our hearts.

For my part, I cannot claim to understand what my daughter was thinking when she reportedly attacked you…

"Reportedly?" Ashland said with a scowl, but I kept reading.

I will always remember you two as the closest of friends and sisters of the heart. Please know that Myron and I love you and hope for the best for you.

If at any point in the future you find information about Mia's claim, please let us know. I'm sure any light you can shed will go a long way in explaining to us what happened to our daughter.

Please call us when you can.

Love, Alice and Myron Reed

"I can't believe this." Ashland's hands were on my shoulder. I clicked off the computer and leaned back in the chair, looking up at him. "Can this be possible? Is she really gone?"

"What I can't believe is that they would ask you to speak at her funeral. Who are these people?"

"That does seem weird—so it's not just me."

He shook his head and said, "Nope. In fact, I bet my attorney would tell you that it could be a trap. Whatever you said could be used as evidence if they chose to try and sue us again."

"You're right. I'm stunned that Mia is dead. I thought she was dead after she attacked me at the house. I thought they were both dead—there was so much blood and…"

"It's okay. You're safe now, and she's really gone this time."

I knew what he was saying was true, but it still didn't seem real. "I don't mean to sound morbid, but I wonder how she died."

"Let's get out of here. Things might get crazy now, especially if the press hears about this. It's best to prepare for whatever publicity firestorm this might create."

"It could get nuts. If Mia was still in that facility, then only one thing could've happened to her—suicide. I would never have imagined that kind of ending for her. She was always so strong-willed, strong-minded. I swear to you, the girl you met wasn't the one I knew. Something happened to her, and I'm not sure what."

"It's no mystery to me, Carrie Jo."

"What?"

"The house got to her. Anyone who comes in contact with that house has had something happen to them. It's like it's cursed or something."

"You don't believe in curses, Ash."

"Two years ago I would have agreed with you. Now I am not so sure." He shook his head. "Are you ready to go home?" I grabbed my purse and followed him to the front door. Chip and Rachel were long gone, so I locked up the building and headed to the car.

"Where are you going? Your car is dead, remember? I'll have the mechanic pick it up tomorrow."

"Yeah, I forgot all about that." Determined to give it a try just once more I said, "Let me just try it." I didn't wait for his answer; I hopped in my BMW and to my surprise it cranked right up. Either there was some glitch with my car or unseen forces were indeed at work—perhaps it wasn't a coincidence that I ended up at that cemetery gate after all.

Ashland pulled up beside me with a frown. "See you at home."

***

When Ashland fell asleep I slipped out of bed. It had started to rain. From the sound of it, the drops were heavy and fat, not the typical pitter-patter drops you hear in spring. Low rumbles of thunder warned of an approaching storm, and I felt an urge to watch it roll in. Mobile had no shortage of springtime storms, but we'd been in kind of a drought recently. Tonight, I could smell the rain in the air.

After having made up from our big blowout about his dreaming, I didn't want to risk invading his privacy again. And I couldn't trust myself not to look. In fact, I really couldn't help it. Just like he couldn't control his dreams, I couldn't control my wandering into them. Gathering up my favorite white quilt, I walked down the hall to the guest room. I flipped on the small lamp by the door just so I didn't trip over anything, I didn't need a lot of light to watch the storm. I shuffled across the wood floor in my socks and plopped in the comfy chaise lounge that overlooked the backyard. It wasn't a fabulous view; there were too many trees and tall buildings to see too much below, but I could see the sky perfectly.

I hunkered down in the chair, wrapped my blanket around me, leaned back and watched the lightning light up the sky. At first the blasts of light were subtle, just flashing through black clouds along the distant horizon. It was a beautiful sight. Then the lightning became more defined. It shot through the massive cloud deck, hitting the dark waters of the bay first and then various spots along the edges of the Port City. Thunder rolled and as it boomed and shook the house, sleep seemed impossible. As I enjoyed the scenery, I protectively rubbed my still flat stomach. I was going to be a mother. Was I ready for that? Well, ready or not, I was going to find out soon. I had no doubt that Ashland would be a good father; he was such a good person. "Good night, little one," I whispered to my stomach. Then I thought about Mia, the sane Mia, the one who would have been delighted to be an aunt. Maybe my husband was right—somehow Seven Sisters had gotten to her, had driven her crazy. Strangely enough I couldn't muster up a single tear.

I rubbed my tired eyes and yawned. The gold-toned pendulum clock on the mantelpiece began to chime. I couldn't believe it was midnight already. I was tired, but I also felt unsettled. I glanced at the side table and the worn copy of *THE STARS THAT FELL*. Could I really afford to stay up half the night reading a book? Well, I *was* the boss. I could call in if I wanted to. I had no appointments that I knew of, so I could certainly sleep late. I tossed my wild curls behind my shoulder and out of my face, picked up the book and turned to the worn silk bookmark.

Okay, Delilah. Help me out here. What's going on in your world, and does it have something to do with mine?

Chapter Nine—Delilah

My second trip to Seven Sisters was no less impressive than my first. The more I thought of it, the more inconceivable it was that I had lived in Mobile most of my life and had never seen this house. But then again that may have been by design. I would never know if my parents, the Iversons, knew about my true identity; however, it did stand to reason that they would want to protect me. Even though my Iverson family would not have cared about what the upper crust of Mobile thought, I did care. I was left alone to fight for my future. Of course, I had choices. Nothing prevented me from moving away from Mobile and its stuffy social circles. At least I had a small fortune that I could fall back on thanks in part to both my families. Still, as I told Jackson Keene, money had nothing to do with my return to Mobile. I came to claim my name and my family. I was secretly heartbroken to learn they did not want to know me at all.

In a strange sort of way, I felt compelled to pursue my name. Partly because, by all accounts, my mother had no choice but to send me away. She was the unhappy wife of a cruel man, a woman who had found some stolen joy in the arms of my father. I liked to think that whatever her flaws were, she loved me deeply and apparently wasn't afraid to stand up to her tormentor when pressed to. I was hoping to learn more about her, my sister and my cousin this afternoon. I pulled up in the carriage and handed the reins to Stokes, the big man who had met us the other night. He was a man of few words and didn't even walk me in, pointing toward the door with a grunt.

Here in the light of day, I could plainly see that Seven Sisters wasn't quite as grand as she used to be. She'd survived demolition during the war, but she hadn't escaped the effects of time and all those stormy summer afternoons. The rain and humidity had left green mold on the columns, and there were loose boards on the porch and missing side rails. Still, it wasn't anything that couldn't be mended if someone had a mind to invest something in the place. I was curious to hear exactly what plans Karah had. Did she plan to sell the house? Deed it to a cousin? I absently wondered if I could afford to buy the place, and if I could (which was doubtable) would I be allowed to do so? I sighed as I climbed the steps carefully.

I did not invite Jackson, as he now insisted that I call him, to return with me. My cousin and I had much to talk about—some privacy should be expected. Better to leave these things within the family. I walked through the open door and followed the sounds of breaking dishes or something. A woman screamed in anger, and I heard another crash. The idea of someone deliberately breaking the beautiful things in this house starched my collar. I stormed down the hall and walked into the Blue Room like I owned the place.

"Put it down now, Docie. I will not tell you again." Karah said, somewhere between tears and anger. "Do not break another thing! You are mad! Just like her!"

Docie grabbed another ceramic dog from the white painted shelf. I looked at the ground in horror. Several other ceramics had already been destroyed; the evidence of Docie's crimes were scattered all around in piles of broken figurines and ceramic dust.

"You don't tell me what to do! I am not your servant but hers!" She raised her hand and prepared to destroy another pup, but I grabbed her arm.

"You break another thing, and I will have you arrested! Put it down now, madam."

So surprised was she that she did as I told her. The ill-tempered Docie dropped the toy dog on the carpeted floor. Luckily for her it did not break. "Now find a broom and dustpan and clean these things up."

With a sneer she brushed past me, pushing her way out of the room. I doubted she would return, but at least her tantrum had ended. "What happened here, Karah? Is she mad? Are you harmed?"

I walked to her, removing my gloves and tossing them and my hat on a nearby settee. "Let me look at you." She seemed frozen and was staring at a spot on the floor. I followed her eyes. She appeared transfixed by one particular ceramic, a cocker spaniel with a red ball in its mouth. "Karah, are you all right?"

She pulled her eyes away and stared into my face. I don't know what I expected to see, but it wasn't the big black bruise around her eye. "Oh my goodness, Karah! Did Docie do this? You need to see a doctor!"

Finally, realization shone across her face. "Delilah?"

"Yes, it's me. You told me to come, remember. What has happened here, Karah?"

"Cousin?"

"Yes. Here and in the flesh." I tried to sound jovial. I still wasn't sure what I was dealing with here. Suddenly she flung her arms around me.

"Thank God. I prayed that you would come. Don't leave me here again. You must stay with me, cousin. I do not think she wants me here, but I want to stay. I have to wait for my mother. She promised she would come! She always keeps her promises! But she...she..." She pointed to the destruction and then sank to the carpet, crying. Yes, there was more here than met the eye.

"Karah, shhh...all is well. See? She is gone, and I will not let her harm you again. Come sit on the couch." Wiping her face on her brown silk dress sleeve she agreed and let me help her up. Before I could question her further, I saw the face of an old, dark-skinned woman peeping in at the door. When she saw me, her yellow eyes widened, and she did not waste any time getting to me.

"I knew that was you, Miss Calpurnia. I said that you would be home soon, and here you are! I am going to have to tell your mother. She will be surprised to hear that you're home—are you home for good? Would you like some tea? You and your friend? Let ol' Hooney get you some tea, just like you like it." So surprised was I that I did not correct her.

"Yes, Hooney. That would be wonderful. Thank you."

She pinched my cheek with her gnarled finger, and I thought she would hug me, but then her face changed. "You ain't Miss Calpurnia." She stepped back in surprise. "Oh, excuse me, miss. I didn't mean to touch you. I just thought you were my mistress's daughter come to see me. I feel like an ol' fool. I guess I won't need to wake up Miss Christine after all."

"No, I am not Calpurnia. But I am her sister, Delilah. Miss Christine was my mother."

Karah had stopped her crying and watched us.

"Oh Lord, can it be true?" Hooney said. "Hannah told me you was okay. But I thought she dropped you somewhere or maybe laid you in the woods. Was you with the doctor? He was a good man, bless him."

"No, he sent me to the Iversons. I had a new family to take care of me, but now I am back. Karah is my cousin." Then inspiration struck me. "What happened to her eye, Hooney? Did the other lady, Docie, do this?"

"Child, I don't know. I heard the commotion and came to see. It could have been her...she's got a mean streak as wide as the Mobile River. But then again, it could have been someone else."

I sat next to my cousin. "Tell me what happened, please."

"I...I..." She started crying again.

I turned to Hooney. "May we have that tea you offered us, Miss Hooney?"

She chuckled. "Oh, it's not Miss. Just Hooney. Yes, ma'am. I'll make you some tea just like the kind your sister liked. Lots of honey."

As she scurried off, I slid the Blue Room door closed behind her and then returned to the settee.

Without waiting for me to ask again, Karah said, "You will never believe me, Delilah. You do not know what has been happening here. It is like the house does not want me here. Things happen. Strange things, and Docie only makes it worse by doing the things she does. She deliberately instigates them."

"Them? Who?"

"The ghosts. The ghosts of Seven Sisters. They don't want me here, but I have to stay. I promised my mother I would wait for her."

I didn't know what to make of her confession. She had been abused, that much was obvious, but ghosts? I never believed in such things. I suspected that if there were any evil entities in this house, they were all very much alive. I sighed and smiled at my cousin. "I'll be here as long as you need me. We will face these ghosts together."

"You promise?"

Trying to bring a lighthearted moment into a very depressing conversation, I raised my hand and said, "I do so promise and swear."

"Very good. We will have Stokes pick up your things, and you can take your sister's room. Let me show it to you. Nothing has been moved since she disappeared. You may find some clues about her there." To my surprise Docie returned to the room with a broom and a dustpan. She did not speak to us but went about her business tidying up the room. We rose to leave but not before I stopped in front of her.

"Everything you have destroyed here today you will replace. You had no right to do so; these belong to my cousin and to me. If you cannot control yourself and keep your temper, then I am sure my cousin can find someone much more suited to this type of home service." Without a word she continued her work and promptly left us. Karah's eyes were wide as she watched me. Suddenly she smiled, which made her face appear much younger. I had only met her a few times but always thought of her as solemn and serious. Her smile was a good reminder that she was young—that we were both young and had our lives ahead of us. "Now come show me this room. I hope it is close to yours."

"It is very close. I am staying in Uncle Louis' room. I must show you his picture—he was a beautiful man. Quite popular with the ladies in Paris and New Orleans. Maybe one day he will turn up with a new bride. Wouldn't that be wonderful?"

"I have never heard of him. You must tell me everything." For the next few hours, we walked through the house. Our tour began in my sister Calpurnia's room. It was a lovely room, but it looked rather sparse without her personal effects in it. Karah told me not to worry and that all of Calpurnia's things were in the armoire. I could look through any of it and keep whatever I liked. Someone in the household, presumably a servant of Calpurnia's, had neatly wrapped up her pretty hair combs, and we found a velvet bag of her necklaces and small rings. My eyes watered just wearing them. To be this close to my sister and now to be with my cousin—the emotion overwhelmed my heart. Next, we went to Louis' trunks and politely peeked inside them. Karah had been correct; Uncle Louis was unusually beautiful, with white skin that appeared to glow, blond hair and beautiful blue eyes. His oil painting likeness portrayed him in a blue blazer with copious blue ruffles, and he looked quite dandy. We put the picture in a respectable place on the downstairs mantelpiece.

"Now, let's go to your mother's room. I am sure you will want to see it."

Suddenly, a quiet reverence washed over me. I nodded and followed her back up the stairs. We walked past Calpurnia's room to the large room on the right. With a sweet smile, Karah opened the door and moved out of the way so I could take in the sight. Instantly I detected the sweet smell of roses. There were none to be seen, but I could smell them nonetheless. "Oh that smell, it's lovely. Where are the roses? Is that a perfume or something?"

Karah sniffed at the air. "I smell nothing, cousin. Perhaps you washed your hands with rosewater earlier. Anyway, I will leave you alone so you can explore your mother's room in peace." Grateful for her thoughtfulness, I nodded as she closed the door quietly. I closed my eyes and then opened them. Here I was at last, in the room where I last saw my mother. I had been an infant then, but now I was a woman. I was suddenly drawn to the bed, my mother's bed. It was large, with a metal rack that hung above it. It was bare now but I was sure that during my mother's time, it had held mosquito netting so the lady of the house could sleep without the incessant buzzing and biting. There was a white cotton quilt on top of it now, and I rubbed my hands across it.

Like a child, I crawled in the bed and clutched the pillow. Loneliness overwhelmed me. They'd all left me. My mother, my father, the Iversons and even my sister Calpurnia. Death had taken them all, except for my sister. I refused to give up hope for her. She would return one day, surely. I cried hot tears of grief, and the loneliness of my soul felt so deep it was as if it were a drum pounding. When I thought I couldn't cry anymore, the smell of roses became stronger and it so comforted me that I fell asleep. I don't know how long I slept, but it could not have been long because the sun was still high in the sky. I heard the sounds of life downstairs, but at least they were happy sounds. No breaking ceramics, no screaming or beatings. It was a happy day.

Suddenly, the light in the room became bright, so bright I could barely see. I shielded my eyes with my hands and tried to discern its source. The light diminished, and in its place was a woman. I knew, somehow I knew, that this woman was my mother. This was Christine Cottonwood.

I sat up and slung my legs over the side of the bed. "Mother?" She didn't answer me. She held a white dress out in front of her and then looked at her reflection in the long mirror. She spun about and laughed. So happy was she!

"Oh! Callie, darling. You startled me. Don't just sit there—come help me change."

"But I am not Callie, Mother. I am Delilah."

"Now, Callie. We do not have time for those kinds of games today. Dr. Page is on his way to take us on a picnic. Come here and hug Mother." I could not resist her request. I sprang to my feet and ran toward her outstretched arms.

"Mother!" The light returned to the room and flared around her body. She smiled still and seemed not to notice the brightness. I shielded my eyes from fear but kept running toward her. She leaned down with a sweet smile, her arms wide, and I ran into them as she disappeared. I was left clutching the air, feeling the last fleeting bits of her leave me alone in her bedroom. The smell of roses faded in a few seconds and was replaced by the smells of a musty old house and my own sweaty body.

"Mother!" I cried out again. The door opened, and Karah stood in the doorway. She looked at me sadly.

"You saw her." It wasn't a question.

"Yes! My mother. I saw her right here. I was in the bed, and then she came in the room with a bright light around her. She thought I was my sister, but I did not care. She tried to hug me. She disappeared." I didn't cry now. I felt comforted, fortunate that I had seen her. I had seen my mother, not just a painting or a photograph. I saw her with my own two eyes, which should have been impossible. My mother was dead.

"They are all here in this house. I see them too. I never wanted to come here, you know." Karah sat on the bed, her feet barely touching the floor. "My mother made me come. She said she would come soon, that I would see her here. But that was four months ago, and I have not heard a word. Not even a letter or a note. I question Docie all the time because I am sure she knows more than she tells me. She is my mother's servant, not mine."

"Well, we shall have to fix that. You are the lady of the house, at least for now. You will have to have your own maid. We can ask Maundy Weaver. She says there are many hardworking French and Irish girls in Mobile looking for work. And I've heard that if you want a secret kept, you can trust an Irish girl. They are extremely loyal."

"I do not have any secrets. Or beaus or anything requiring a maid. I am just the bastard child of Isla Beaumont and Jeremiah Cottonwood. There—I said it! I am a bastard."

Absently I squeezed her hand. "I am too. Let's not use that name anymore. We are more than a name."

She smiled weakly. "Agreed."

I had to ask her more questions. "Tell me, Karah. You say they are all here in this house. Who are you talking about? Who have you seen?" I no longer doubted that she saw ghosts at Seven Sisters.

"Well, I have seen my father in the room across from the Blue Room, I think it was his study. I have seen a young black woman in the downstairs larder. She pulls my hair and scares me to death. Then I have seen other people, people I do not know. I have looked through all the pictures and cannot identify them. Will you help me? Will you keep me safe?"

"I think we need to call the priest. I hear there is a new priest in Mobile now, a Father Portier. No doubt he would come and pray for us."

"I don't think bastard children are allowed to take communion, cousin."

"We won't ask for it. Surely he would not be opposed to offering a few prayers on our behalf. We are after all very wealthy women."

"Perhaps you are right. But just in case, may I sleep with you tonight? Nothing evil has happened here, has it?"

I was quiet for a moment. I felt nothing but peace and happiness in this room. If something evil had occurred here, my mother's love for her children had washed it all away.

"You can sleep in my bed if you promise not to snore."

"Oh, thank you, cousin."

I hugged her, happy that she felt safe with me.

"I do still intend to work with Maundy, though. I hope you understand that I cannot be here every day all the time. I have to keep my commitments, and I will need to explain to my brother—I mean to Adam."

"I see. I would like to meet your brother sometime, cousin."

I blushed at that idea. I was sure that Adam would be charming—too charming for his own good or for Karah's. I determined quietly to never let that happen. I would tell him nothing. Did he deserve anything more from me? "We shall see, cousin."

She smiled, and we spent the rest of the afternoon walking around the house and waiting for Stokes to return with my things. I also jotted off a note to Jackson asking him to wait on finding my house. I now had a place to stay, at least for a little while. The day ended pleasantly, albeit strangely. This wasn't where I had intended to lay my head at night when I woke this morning, but it felt right.

My favorite part of each day would be when she and I lay in bed together and whispered late into the night. We saw no ghosts, not that first night. It felt as if we were sisters, two cast-off sisters who had finally found one another. I was grateful for that. I was grateful for her. She had no reason to show me such favor, but she did. For the first time in a long time, I fell asleep feeling like I was at home—at last.

Chapter Ten—Henri

The Stuarts were on their way—I was looking forward to seeing my friends. I intended to tell them about Detra Ann, if they hadn't already heard that she was leaving, and hopefully enlist their help in getting her to stay. Yes, I had selfish reasons for wanting to keep her in Mobile, but I was also worried about her. She was drinking every day—something she had always hated as long as I'd known her.

Now Lenore referred to her as "the ghost," and that really disturbed me. Detra Ann had cheated death in a very real way...what if Lenore was right? What if the supernatural world wasn't finished with her yet? Moving to another city wouldn't prevent any such encounter. Now how to convey that to her?

I didn't cook this evening, but I had made a few appetizers and mixed a pitcher of hurricanes. Not the syrupy red drink that looked like Kool-Aid, but the authentic New Orleans drink. Lenore, in a rare happy mood, offered to help and even wore a dress for the occasion. I said nothing about her out-of-style baggy denim dress or her mismatched socks. No need to look a gift horse in the mouth, right?

"I think I hear a car."

"Okay, I'll go check." I opened the door and saw Carrie Jo's car in my driveway. The couple stepped out, and CJ waved to me. I waved back and stood on the porch drying my hands on a dish towel.

"Hey, Henri!" Carrie Jo bounded up the steps and hugged me tight. "I am so happy to see you."

"Likewise." I smiled and kissed her cheek and hugged Ashland.

"How's it going, Henri? Things good at the shop?"

"More than good. Come in. I want you to meet my cousin, Lenore."

Lenore flashed a friendly smile, and after everyone exchanged pleasantries I invited them to sit in the living room. "Who wants a drink? I made a batch of hurricanes."

"I'll take one," Ashland piped up. "I guess that means you're driving," he said to Carrie Jo.

Carrie Jo smiled. "I think I can handle that."

"You don't want even a small glass? I use a brown sugar base. It's delicious."

"I have no doubt about that, Henri, but I'm still going to have to pass." The smile on her face told me she wasn't telling me something. She looked at Ashland and said, "Can I tell him?" Her husband nodded, and she smiled even bigger. "Ashland and I are going to be parents."

"Really? That is the best news I've heard in a long time. Congratulations, you two. When is the baby due to arrive?"

"Sometime in May. My doctor says we'll know for sure at the next appointment. I still can't believe it—I'm going to be a mom!" Lenore congratulated them, and we celebrated with a toast. Lemonade for CJ and hurricanes for the rest of us.

"And it's going to be a boy. A boy that looks just like his daddy. A fine healthy young man." Lenore wrapped her hands around her crossed knees and nodded confidently at the couple. Carrie Jo was too polite to say anything except thank you.

"Well, whatever it is, boy or girl, we hope it's just one. I don't think I could handle twins. Especially if they were twin boys."

Lenore shook her head as if she had something to say, but I quickly changed the subject.

"Have either of you spoken to Detra Ann recently?"

"Not me. What about you, Ashland?"

Ashland sipped his drink and shook his head. "She's not returning my calls. I visited her mom recently, and she hasn't seen much of her either. I was hoping you could give us some insight. What's going on with her?"

Lenore let out a little hiss, and I shot her a warning look. "We had dinner the other night. She brought me a little birthday gift—it was the key to the shop. She's moving to Atlanta and leaving me Cotton City Treasures. Everything happened so fast I didn't ask her too many questions because she seemed like she was in a hurry to leave. I'm worried about her."

"You should be. The girl is a shade—she's a ghost already."

Carrie Jo set her lemonade on the table and turned to look at Lenore. "What do you mean, Lenore?"

"I mean the girl has touched Death. She's been in its presence, and it thinks it has a claim on her. It took her friends, and it should have taken her too, but somehow she resisted it. I can promise you that won't last—Death will not be denied. I'm sorry for your friend, but it is the truth."

I tried to keep my voice level. "You don't know what you're talking about. I've asked you to stop talking about Detra Ann like that."

"It's not my fault that you love a ghost, Henri, but I can't lie. She's marked, and she'll pass on soon. And there ain't nothing you can do about it. I am sorry, but it's the honest-to-God truth." She took a big swig of her drink and licked her lips. "I haven't had one of these good drinks in a long time. Pour me another one."

Carrie Jo's eyes were wide with fear. "You can't be right about this. I don't mean to be rude, but what are you basing your statement on? I don't know if you know it or not, but we've been battling the supernatural here in Mobile for over a year and a half. We've seen our share of ghosts and we've beaten them—Detra Ann too. I don't think you realize how strong she is. This can't be true."

Lenore surprised us all by scooting closer to Carrie Jo and taking her hand in hers. She patted it and spoke to her in a soothing voice. "I am sorry that I offended you. I know something about battling the supernatural too. I guess Henri hasn't told you that I've been doing it all my life. People think I'm crazy, and maybe that's true, but there are patterns—laws that the supernatural world follows. Death is hard to escape, especially if it knows what you look like. I'm sure that your Detra Ann is a wonderful person, that she doesn't deserve this, but that doesn't change the fact that she is in danger. Big-time danger."

"If what you say is true, that Death will come for her, then it will come for me too because I was with her. We fought this together. I refuse to abandon her now."

"Maybe you should tell me exactly what happened. If you don't mind. Don't leave anything out. Even small things can help."

For the next hour, Ashland and Carrie Jo caught her up. I shared any relevant bits that they missed but otherwise kept quiet. I was learning a lot too. For example, I never knew about Carrie Jo's dream about Jeremiah Cottonwood and his vicious whip. How unusual that she woke up with the stripe of his whip on her leg. Ashland told us about his first encounter with Isla, and Carrie Jo shared her first dream about Calpurnia Cottonwood. Then we talked about the Moonlight Garden, the treasure, the ghosts of Jeremiah and David Garrett. They told her about the loss of Bette and Terrence Dale, how they saw Hoyt Page and Delilah and Christine. By the end of it, she had more questions, and we answered them as best we could.

"Well, it's obvious that Mobile is a hot spot for the supernatural and that Seven Sisters seems to be ground zero. Everything that's happened to you all has centered around that house. But first, let's deal with the practical things." Lenore took Carrie Jo's hands and stared at them. "Hmm...I never was any good at that. Palm reading, I mean. Let me look into your eyes." She didn't wait to be invited. She grabbed Carrie Jo's wrists and stared deep into her eyes. I almost said something, but Ashland gave me a reassuring look.

Lenore continued, "I know what you say is true about the battle you and Detra Ann did, but she's the shade—not you. No ghost in there. I see only you. As far as your dream catching goes, before you go to sleep at night, you have to put the baby to sleep." Carrie Jo laughed, but Lenore pressed on. "Your little one is who is causing you to wander into your husband's dreams. That little boy will have the same powers his mother does, and maybe some of his father's too. He is already dreaming about you and his daddy. You know more than you think you do, Mrs. Stuart. You didn't have any problems before this, did you? I mean, you could sleep with your husband and drift right off to sleep, right?"

"Yes, that's true."

"It's the baby. He can't control his powers—he doesn't even understand that he has them and that he is special. For a good night's sleep, eat something bland before bed, no sodas or sugar, and sing to him. Sing until he goes to sleep. Then you can sleep without worry."

Carrie Jo nodded uncertainly but then smiled. "It's better than anything I've come up with. I will give it a try."

Then Lenore turned her attention to Ashland. "Start telling your wife the truth about the things you see. Like when you saw that man in the car window…"

"I didn't tell anyone about that." Ashland seemed surprised, and pink rose under his tanned skin.

"It's written on your face. You need to tell her, and you two have to work as a team. I don't know what you have going in your life, but you need to make room for your gift—stop being ashamed of it. It's not going away, and it is only going to get stronger, so be prepared for that. Ask God to help you."

"How do I do that?" He looked confused.

"That's up to you. Go out on your boat and reconnect with Him. He'll help you. He will, I promise."

"So there's no way to make this stop?"

She shook her head emphatically.

"Do I talk to these things or what?"

"You can try, but I doubt they will say anything coherent—just look at what they look at. Pay attention to details. You won't be able to help all of them, but you may be able to help some of them find their rest. I don't have all the answers, but I know pretending it's not happening is not a strategy that works." She touched his cheek, and he didn't back away. "One more thing, Ashland…"

"Yes. What is it?"

"You don't know it all yet. There's something you haven't figured out. You haven't seen the complete truth, the whole truth, the so-help-you-God truth yet. Be prepared for it because the truth won't be denied."

She turned to me with sad eyes. "Now I come to you, Henri Devecheaux. It has been too long since you said her name. She wonders why you do not pray for her, talk to her, look for her. I feel her around this place. Can you see her, Ashland?"

"Not yet, but I sense that someone is very near to Henri." He stared behind me and then shook his head. "No, she's gone."

"That's because you haven't been looking for her." It was more than a statement. It was an accusation. I felt ashamed and angry that she would bring up this subject right now. "You have to find her, Henri. Find her and bring her home so she can rest in peace. When you do, you'll have peace yourself."

I stood up and glared at Lenore. "What if I don't want to know what happened? What good will it do? That was over twenty years ago, Lenore. Am I supposed to spend every day of my life looking for her? I loved her, but she's gone now and I have to let her go—so do you. You have to! I have to! I'll go crazy if I think about it. Is that what you want? Me talking crazy, locked up somewhere?"

"Aleezabeth! Aleezabeth! Can't you even say her name? Quit calling her 'she' and 'her.' She was a living, breathing person—someone you loved!"

"Fine! Aleezabeth! Are you happy?"

Ashland waved his hand. "Um, guys. You said to start sharing. You have a visitor. Tall, olive-skinned girl with long brown hair, a pink skirt, pink knee socks and some kind of white school shirt. She's in the corner of the room. She's barely there." He pointed toward the fireplace as if he were pointing at a clock or a picture, not a ghost. "Can you see her?"

"No, I can't," I said sharply, suddenly afraid.

"Say something to her, Henri." Lenore stood beside me and faced the fireplace.

"I didn't know this would happen. I did not mean for this to happen. I should have stayed with you…" My voice broke, and my heart felt like a rock. "I should have stayed with you. I am sorry, Aleezabeth." I sat on the couch and leaned across the arm, crying. Lenore stared at the corner of the room as if she could see her, and perhaps she could. I could not, but I did feel better.

Ashland gave me a sad smile. "She's gone. I guess that was all she needed to hear—at least for now. I am sorry, Henri. I never knew that you lost someone like that."

I rubbed my eyes with a tissue that Carrie Jo stuffed in my hand. I took a big swig of my hurricane and said, "It isn't something I like to think about too much. I have a life now. I want to keep moving forward, not backward."

He nodded. "I am living proof that sometimes you have to look back to move forward."

Someone knocked on the front door, and I excused myself to answer it. I heard a pretty voice on the front porch and recognized it right away—it was Detra Ann. "Avon calling. Are y'all having a party without me?" I opened it, and she nearly fell inside laughing. It was immediately apparent that she was at least three sheets to the wind. "You know, you really would make a lousy boyfriend. You don't call, you don't come over. That's pretty lousy, Henri." She stumbled into the living room, her red high heels in her hand. "Hey, everyone. I know y'all. Except you. I don't know you—but hey anyway! What are we celebrating? Ooh…are those hurricanes?"

Lenore stepped backward, never taking her eyes off Detra Ann, until she left the room completely.

"Was it something I said?"

"No, that's just Lenore. I don't think you need any hurricanes, Detra Ann. How about some coffee?"

"Whatever you say, doctor." She kissed me on the cheek. I could smell bourbon—it must have been tonight's choice at the bar. "Call me doc-tor love…" she sang off-key and loudly.

"Where have you been tonight, Detra Ann?" I heard Ashland ask as I made a quick pot of coffee.

"Dancing, drinking and saying goodbye to Mobile. I am going to miss this place and all of you. I love y'all, but I have to go." I could hear the stress in her voice now. "I can't stay here, or something bad will happen. I can feel it. You wouldn't understand. I know I should have told you sooner, but my heart couldn't handle it. Yep, my heart…I love you all." Then she began to sing again, "I can feel your heart beat—the heart of love…. Hey! Wasn't that one of your favorite songs, Carrie Jo? That guy William could sing—the band covered all his songs. But don't tell Ashland—I don't think he'd like hearing that too much." I cringed as she rambled on, oblivious to the fact that Ashland was sitting right there. "Hey, where did that girl go? Is that the mysterious cousin—is that your cousin, Henri? I don't think she likes me too much."

"Do you want cream and sugar?" I called to her from the kitchen.

"I want bourbon!"

"You aren't getting any," I replied, shaking my head. At least now I didn't have to explain her drinking problem to Carrie Jo and Ashland. Lenore was right, I sure could pick them. But I couldn't help loving Detra Ann. I poured some of the hot chicory coffee in a stoneware mug, walked into the living room and handed it to her. She thanked me with a pout.

"Ow, that's hot."

Carrie Jo was staring at Ashland. I looked too and saw his face was as white as a sheet. He stared at the front door, and my arms began to feel cold and clammy.

"What is it, Ash?" she whispered.

"I am not sure, but come get behind me. The whole doorway is full of blackness—it's crawling all over the doorframe. Can anyone else see it?"

We all looked, except Detra Ann, who was slow to comprehend the increasing danger. She just stared at us. "What?"

"I can't see it, but I can feel something," I confessed. I sat next to Detra Ann and put my arm around her protectively. Lenore was long gone. *Yeah, battling the supernatural. Right. More like running from it.*

"Carrie Jo, Ashland is right. You need to get behind him—better still, go down the hall." Suddenly frightened, Carrie Jo got to her feet in a flash and would have pulled Detra Ann with her, but I stopped her. "No, leave her with us. We can't risk it following her. We'll stay with her. You go!"

I heard Lenore whisper to her, and Carrie Jo disappeared.

Ashland spoke in a low voice. "That's nothing I have ever seen before, Henri. It's a shape now and he's tall, taller than anyone I have ever known and completely inky black. Oh my God! Do you feel that? It's like all the oxygen just left the room. I think Lenore is right—this is Death we are dealing with."

Detra Ann sobered in an instant. She put down the cup of coffee and clung to me.

"You feel it too? I'm not crazy then?"

"No, you're not. What do we do, Henri? Should I say something?"

"Say nothing," I whispered fiercely. "Be still and pray, both of you. Close your eyes and pray right now!" We did just that. Detra Ann whispered some words, Ashland said the Lord's Prayer aloud, and I poured out my heart to heaven. "God please, protect the woman I love and my friends. She cannot leave yet. Her time is not up. Please, if you have to take someone, take me." My eyes wanted to open, and it was a struggle to keep them closed, but I kept praying, probably louder than I intended. Soon the room felt different. The ominous presence vanished, and the air felt alive again. One by one we opened our eyes. Ashland told us the shape had disappeared. With shaking hands, Detra Ann picked up her coffee. When she realized her hands were too shaky to do her any good, she set it back down on the table.

"It doesn't matter where I go, does it? It is going to follow me. It wants me, I know it. Am I going to die, Henri?"

"We are going to fight, Detra Ann. You won't die—I will be with you the whole time. I swear."

"Can I stay with you?"

"Of course you can." She put her arms around me, and for the first time ever I kissed her. A real kiss, not a friendly, can-I-be-your-pal kiss. She didn't run away or laugh in my face. She kissed me back. I had never been so terrified and so happy in such a short space of time.

That was the moment Lenore chose to step out of the hallway. "Well if she's staying here, I'm leaving. I can't stay with a ghost."

"That's fine with me, Lenore. I didn't ask you to move in."

Detra Ann laughed. "I am not a ghost. I was just drunk, that's all. I am sorry you had to see me like that."

"It ain't the booze, sister—it's the specter following you around. He ain't fixin' to grab me. No way, no how."

She crossed her arms stubbornly and stared at me with a perfectly arched eyebrow.

Carrie Jo said sweetly, "Lenore, you can stay with Ashland and me. We have a guest room. I'd like to have you around—maybe you can help us learn what we need to know." I could almost hear her say, "And Henri and Detra Ann could have some time to catch up." She smiled at Ashland, who nodded in agreement.

"Okay, then. Let me get my stuff. Be right back." Lenore left only to return a minute later. "This is it. I don't have much."

"That's great. Well, thank you for the drinks, Henri. I think we'll be going home now. Let's talk in the morning. We have to come up with some sort of plan."

Lenore waited on the porch, still refusing to stay in the room with Detra Ann. I hoped she behaved herself during her stay with the Stuarts. With Lenore, anything was possible. And I hadn't forgotten her mysterious phone call.

I found one…

Chapter Eleven—Carrie Jo

By the time we made it home I realized how impulsive I had been inviting a complete stranger into our home. But I soothed my nervousness by reminding myself that it was for Henri and Detra Ann. I had privately been rooting for them, and it just made sense to see them get together now. Nobody could ever take Terrence Dale's place, but I couldn't help but believe he would want Detra Ann to be happy. Hopefully Ashland agreed with me; he had to see how good she and Henri could be for one another.

Lenore didn't talk on the drive back to our home. I was dying to ask Ashland about what he saw at Henri's, but I wasn't in the mood to hear Lenore declare Detra Ann a ghost again. When we pulled into the driveway, Lenore didn't move right away. I got out of the car and waited on her. "Are you coming, Lenore?"

She was watching the house, her penetrating eyes examining the exterior for God only knew what. Slowly she opened the car door and stepped outside clutching her two Wal-Mart bags that overflowed with her colorful wardrobe. I sighed and walked up the sidewalk. She'd either come inside or she wouldn't. Ashland opened the door and gave me an amused look. "I know, I know," I whispered.

Eventually she did come in and was the perfect houseguest. I showed her the guest room, guest bathroom and kitchen, telling her to grab something to eat if she got hungry. "What are your plans tomorrow? Are you working somewhere? Do you need a lift?"

"No. I have applications out, but nobody has called me yet. I don't suppose you need a housekeeper or something?"

"No. We have a housekeeper. You will probably meet her tomorrow. Her name is Doreen, and she makes an awesome…well, everything. But if you're interested in that type of work, she might be able to tell you where to go. I bet with the approaching Mardi Gras festivities you could find a job easily."

"That might work," she said, looking hopeful.

"I am going to the office in the morning, but you tell Doreen what you're looking for. If she can't help you, we'll look somewhere else."

Her face softened, and she smiled. "Thank you. That means a lot."

"Good night, Lenore."

"Good night."

I closed the door and went upstairs to pass out. It didn't happen—Ashland was keyed up and ready to talk about what he'd seen. In fact, he wanted to tell me about everything he'd seen. If Lenore helped no one else, she had helped Ash. Sure, she was quirky, but underneath I could tell she had true empathy for people. Plus, she claimed to know a great deal about the supernatural world, and Henri didn't dispute her knowledge. If anyone knew the truth about her, it would have been him.

She seemed like a lost child, wandering through the world depending on the kindness of strangers. She was friendly to everyone...except Detra Ann. I wondered why that was. Perhaps she was jealous of Henri's blooming relationship, or maybe she opposed the idea of her cousin involved with someone ten years younger—or someone white.

Ashland continued talking, and I nodded attentively. He described the ghost man he saw in the car, the many ghosts in the windows of the houses along Conception Street, even the creepy one he used to see regularly when his mother took him to Sunday brunch at the Admiral Semmes Hotel. I listened patiently, pretending that I wasn't creeped out. The poor guy. I couldn't imagine seeing stuff like that all the time and then forcing myself to forget it just to keep my sanity.

I stifled a yawn. I seemed to have no energy today. Boy, missing those pre-natal vitamins even for a day made a difference. I undressed as he talked and finally slid on his old football jersey. I had silk nightgowns aplenty but couldn't resist sleeping in oversize shirts—especially ones that smelled like Ashland's expensive cologne.

"That's not fair."

I folded back the coverlet and slid under the sheets. "What's not fair?"

"You...undressing right now."

I rubbed scented lotion on my hands and feigned innocence. "I have no idea what you're talking about."

He was undressing too and was under the sheets with me in a few seconds. "I love you, Carrie Jo Stuart. I can't imagine spending my life with anyone else."

"That's a good thing, 'cause I feel the same way."

"Say it, then."

I kissed his perfect lips and whispered, "I love you, Ashland Stuart."

For the next hour, we lost ourselves in one another, totally uncaring that someone else was in the house. Afterwards, Ashland dozed off to sleep, but our lovemaking had the opposite effect on me tonight—I couldn't close my eyes. I decided a nice long shower and maybe then a snack would help settle me down. If the butterflies in my stomach were any indication, the baby approved of that idea. After drying off and pulling my hair on top of my head in a messy bun, I padded down the stairs to see what treats Doreen had left me. I was happy to see that she left me a container of mandarin orange fruit salad topped with sweetened pecans. It may not have been comfort food for some folks, but ever since I got pregnant I couldn't get enough of the citrus fruit. Taking the whole container, a spoon and a bottle of water, I slipped into my office and quietly closed the door behind me.

After a few spoonfuls of the tasty treat, I flipped on my laptop in hopes of seeing an email from Desmond Taylor. Nope, nothing yet. I deleted a bunch of junk mail until just the important stuff was left. Digging into the fruit salad, I reread the email from the Reeds. Of course I wasn't going to go to Mia's funeral, but it wouldn't do any good to be mean about it. I felt sorry for Alice and Myron, even though they had considered suing Ashland and me. I wrote them back thanking them for the honor but declining their invitation without giving them a specific reason why. That would have to do. I hit send with a sigh and deleted their original email. That was easier than I'd thought it would be. I hoped that would be the end of the whole sad situation.

Goodbye, Mia.

On a whim, I searched for Father Portier and the Cathedral Basilica of the Immaculate Conception. An image of the friendly white-haired priest appeared. It was the picture of an oil painting—a commemorative portrait from 1829 marking Portier's appointment as the first bishop of Mobile. I could hardly believe it. I had a full-on conversation with a ghost, and I hadn't been asleep. I saved the photo and dug deeper into the history of the cathedral. How was it that I had walked through the gate and ended up in the church three blocks over unless I somehow stumbled into some sort of supernatural portal? Was there such a thing? It had been a common practice in the 1700s and 1800s to build churches atop old religious centers. It was actually a common way to show the natives who the new boss was. I continued to read until my stomach was full and my eyes began to glaze.

That's enough. I need to rest.

I closed the laptop, leaned back in my chair and spun around to enjoy the view of the moonlight bouncing around the backyard. Our little house was quiet except for the occasional sounds of a beam creaking. That sort of thing was to be expected in a home this old. But then I heard another sound, someone talking. It was quiet but distinct. As silently as possible, I went to my door and opened it. Lenore was talking to someone, and from the tone of her voice she was frantic.

"No, I can't do that. You don't understand...I don't know what you mean...."

I knew it was an invasion of her privacy, but I crept into the hallway and stood outside her door. If Lenore was going to do something crazy in my house, I wanted to know about it. I held my breath and took a peek. She had the house phone up to her ear and was sitting on the bed in her pajamas. Her hair looked wild and unbrushed, as if she'd just woken up.

"Why are you asking me to do this? You know I love you..."

Hearing her move around the room, I leaned flush against the wall. *That's enough of that, Carrie Jo. Now go to bed and quit snooping.*

I sprinted down the hall in my sock feet and slid through the open door of my office. I closed the container of fruit salad and put the lid back on my water. I paused to slow my pounding heartbeat.

Lenore's whispering continued, and my hand went protectively to my stomach. I couldn't let it go. I had to know what was going on. Who was she talking to at this time of night, and why was she so upset? My hand rested on the old-fashioned princess phone on my desk. Should I? What if she was in danger? It sounded like someone was trying to convince her to do something she did not want to do. As quietly as I could, I picked up the phone just to make sure Lenore was okay.

"I'm not ready...I can't do it...yes...I understand. I know what this means. This is forever, ain't it?"

There was nobody there—just Lenore speaking into the phone, the dial tone buzzing in the background. With a lump in my throat I put the phone down, left the food on my desk and slinked out of the room. All I wanted to do now was brush my teeth, go to bed and cuddle as closely to Ashland as I could.

This couldn't be good.

Chapter Twelve—Delilah

As the weeks flew by, the excitement in Mobile grew almost to fever pitch. The city's hotels were filling up as dignitaries and curious visitors from the surrounding counties descended on the downtown area. Lampposts were festooned with purple and gold ribbon, but the city held back a bit on some of the festivities, remembering to honor their war dead with the appropriate decorum. The lost "sons of the south" would be honored during the first parade with an Ash Processional. Relatives of the lost would march in silence dressed in black and doused in ashes, and Maundy and I had spent all morning sewing black ribbons to sell to the supporters. According to Honoree Daughtry, the wife of the commissioner responsible for this year's Mardi Gras activities, this event was expected to help the city begin to "heal from its wounds." I thought the whole thing was morbid, but it kept my hands busy and my mind off my situation.

Parade watchers were already lining the streets and covered the walkways like flies on a watermelon carcass prepared to fully enjoy Mobile's Mardi Gras opening spectacle. We quickly sold our baskets of ribbons, and I took the empty containers back to the shop while Maundy stayed behind to watch.

From what she told me, festivities like the debutante auction and the Night of Masks ball were quite decadent. I wondered what the austere Miss Claudette Page would think about those. I was certain that she would be staging a rally against this sort of revelry, but in fact, Miss Page was a former Boeuf Gras Society queen. Although that mystical organization had dissolved right before the Civil War, Claudette continued to work on behalf of many such organizations. To my disappointment, that had been the most scandalous tidbit I had learned about my estranged aunt thus far. As my court date approached, I began to see my chances of persuading Miss Page to acquiesce to my father's will all but disappear. Perhaps Maundy's idea of gathering information on her had been a waste of my time, just a ruse to hire a decent dressmaker. Thus far, Maundy had gotten much more information from me than I had from her. She pressed me all the time about Adam, leaving me with no doubt that she had was interested in him.

As I pushed my way through the crowd, I reflected on the past few weeks. There had seemed no end to the line of women that flowed through Maundy's parlor and dress shop. We worked as fast as our fingers would allow us, sometimes late into the night. Karah had gotten into the habit of sending the Brougham carriage around to pick me up at five o'clock, which was a blessing. But many was the night when Stokes had to wait for me, sometimes for hours. Regardless of the time of my return, my cousin would be there in the Blue Room with a plate of food and a smile, eager to hear about my day at Mobile's busiest dress shop. I often invited her to visit me at the shop, to come get to know Maundy and the other women I worked with, but she always refused, saying that she did not want to miss her mother's arrival. I pointed out that her mother was not set to arrive for a few days, but she said that she wouldn't put it past her to arrive early.

After all these weeks of being with Karah, I knew very little about her mother other than that she was a popular and gifted actress and quite a beauty. Karah showed me handbills with her image and even shared a tiny portrait of her in a locket that Karah wore about her neck. From what I could see, Karah looked very much like her only thinner and not nearly as flamboyantly dressed. I did not feel anxious about her arrival. I assumed that anyone related to Karah would be kind and friendly.

During one of my late nights at work Adam came by the shop, but Maundy sent him away. She told him we were rushed to finish ball gowns and could not be bothered with a social visit. Listening on the other side of the parlor door, I heard the entire conversation. Maundy was polite but firm in her refusal to let him see me, yet she invited him to visit her for dinner after Mardi Gras ended. I said nothing when she returned but tucked the information away for later use.

The following evening I arrived at Seven Sisters as usual, tired and hungry, but I immediately knew something was wrong. Karah wasn't at her usual place at the round cherrywood table that we often used for our late-night suppers. She was thumbing through one of the many books of poems in the ladies' parlor and barely noticed when I arrived. A stack of books was beside her on the table and I could tell she was looking for something important.

"Good evening, cousin," I said pleasantly and reached for the plate that Hooney left for me. The bread was dry and the soup was cold, but I was so hungry it didn't matter. I dipped the bread into the oniony broth and snacked away.

She turned around, her face in a book, then looked up and gasped. "Oh goodness. What time is it?"

"It's nearly nine o'clock. I didn't mean to startle you. I spoke, but you were immersed in your book. Must be an interesting read."

"I was just…well, you're here now."

"Yes, and I think this is the last late night for me, unless Mrs. Broadus brings her daughter's dress back for some reason or another—which wouldn't surprise me in the least. The way that young lady puts on weight is astonishing. Is there something I can help you find?"

She shook her head and placed the book on top of the others in the nearby stack. Docie walked in, scowled at me and walked back out. Looking even more uncomfortable, Karah said, "Please excuse Docie. She's not used to socializing with other people."

I wiped the crumbs from my hands and said, "Why do you keep her, Karah? She isn't only unpleasant, she also is dangerous and has no regard for our family's things. Not to mention how abominably she treats you. I do not understand. Surely you can find another maid."

She shrugged and absently ran her finger across the spine of the book. Since she was content to stare at her hands, I asked, "What is it? I can see that something is on your mind. Is it your mother? Should I leave?"

"No, I do not want you to go. I think when she meets you she will like you, just as I do. But the truth is my mother is very changeable and I am never too good at predicting her thoughts or her moods. That's not what has me puzzled, though."

"Oh? What is it?" My eyes hurt, and my fingers felt stiff and dry, but I waited to hear her revelation.

"Adam Iverson came by Seven Sisters today."

I sat up straighter and began to apologize. "I will speak with him. I promise he won't come back again. Did he behave inappropriately?"

My lovely cousin pursed her lips in thoughtful expression. The ivory candles on the table sputtered on their shiny candlesticks. I felt an unmistakable draft in the room. The flickering flames cast strange shadows on the wall beside us. "He is in love with you, I think." I could not hide my surprise at her observation. "Mr. Iverson is unashamedly flirtatious, but all he wanted to talk about was you. Do you love him, Delilah? He is rather handsome in a rugged, farmhand sort of way."

"I…" I felt my skin warm, and I toyed with my bread.

Karah quickly added, "Perhaps your affections lie somewhere else now, as Mr. Iverson seems to believe."

How would I navigate this turn in conversation? Until tonight, Karah had never asked me about Adam or our relationship, and I was too tired to play parlor games with her. My rebellious heart won over the intelligent part of my mind that encouraged me to tread lightly.

"I loved him as a brother, until I knew he was not my brother. I thought he felt the same way about me."

"So he mistreated you? Took advantage of you?" She tilted her head and folded her hands in front of her on the table. Seeing my hesitation, she poured me another glass of water.

"No, not intentionally. Adam cannot be anything but who he is. I think we were naïve—I was naïve—but there were no promises made. I had no promise."

"You yielded yourself to him?" Karah leaned forward, the tiny lines on her forehead deepening as she whispered. I sipped my water and did not answer her but merely gave her a glum look. She obviously had never been in love. "What about Jackson? Are you interested in him, Delilah? Not to be crass, cousin, but I do not know any other way to ask."

Surprised by the question I unthinkingly blurted an answer. "Mr. Keene and I have a business relationship. I consider him a friend but only a friend."

"Then you would not mind if he called on me?"

"I have no reason to object."

She reached across the table and squeezed my hand happily. "I am so pleased to hear that. Forgive me for being so forward, cousin. I just had to know. If I thought you had your cap set for him, I would never encourage his attention. I have strong feelings on this matter. I never want to be accused of competing with my dear cousin. There are too many men in the world for that."

I smiled back at her, pretending to be happy. Why hadn't I told her the truth, that I was not sure how I felt about Mr. Keene? Now it was too late say so. Quietly I internalized the meaning of all this. Because of my confession, Karah now knew all about my involvement with Adam and she made it plain she had designs on our attorney. Maundy was right—I was too quick to speak my mind.

"Did you hear me, Delilah?"

"Yes," I lied, then took a sip of my water. I did not drink often, but I suddenly felt the need for a glass of wine or some of Maundy's strong drink.

"Really? What did I say?"

"I apologize, Karah. I guess I am more tired than I thought." I stood up and stretched my sore back.

"It wasn't important. We can talk tomorrow. Can I count on you to help me get the house ready for Mother tomorrow? I want everything to look its best. I am sure Maundy can spare you one day."

"Yes, I will gladly help you. I think I will go to bed now. Do you need help finding your lost bookmark?"

"Bookmark?"

"Yes, or whatever it is you are looking for." I pointed to the messy stack of dusty books piled on the table.

"Oh, bookmark. No, I think I will retire too in just a few minutes. It *is* getting late. Good night, cousin."

"Good night, Karah." Feeling unhappy, I left her in the ladies' parlor and walked down the hall toward the staircase. No candles had been lit in the hallway, and the entire top floor was like a yawning black cavern. The hem of my blue dress had torn as I stepped out of the carriage earlier. I would need to repair it, but now I just wanted to prevent myself from tripping over it and tumbling up or down the stairs. I picked up my skirts to climb up to Calpurnia's room when an odd amber-colored light shining in from the glass door to the Moonlight Garden caught my eye. I paused to decide if I should call out to Karah, but the events of the evening still stung. I decided to have a look myself. It was not unusual to see lights on the property at night, but the color of the light attracted my attention. I had never seen anything like it. As I walked toward the door, the light moved away from the garden entrance, but I could plainly see it shining through the trees.

I opened the door and hoped to avoid waking Stokes, who slept in the small room under the stairs. He was an odd man—an empty man who did not enjoy idle chitchat, especially with women. From what Karah whispered to me on the few occasions we had the opportunity to speak without enduring Docie's disapproving stares, Stokes had been Mr. Cottonwood's right-hand man, never too far from his master. I wondered what the former slave thought about me—if he even knew or cared who I was. The door clicked behind me, and I stepped out on the brick walkway.

Karah and I had walked through the garden during my initial tour of the home, but there had been plenty of daylight to see by. In the day it was a marvelous place, full of hidden spots for reading a book or, as Karah put it, stealing a kiss. But it seemed a forlorn place at night. It was completely dark, with the exception of the half-moon above me and the odd amber light hovering on the other side of the trees.

I walked the half circle to the opening of the maze path, pausing to see if I could determine the source of the light. Tendrils from my usually neat bun slapped my face as a blast of wind blew through the garden, almost pulling me down the path. My hand flew up to shield my face from an unexpected shower of damp magnolia leaves. Then I heard my name whispered on the breeze, "Delilah, Delilah."

"Who's there?" I asked in a near whisper. My heart was pounding in my chest as if I had run through the whole garden. My skin tingled, and my lips felt dry. I stopped on the path, my mind torn between the choices—run back to the house or continue my search to determine the source of the unusual light. "Who's there?" I said in a stronger voice. The wind blew steadily, but at least the trees were not pelting me with foliage. Shielding my eyes with my hand, I watched the light bounce further into the maze. Curiosity won the battle with fear, and I pressed on. In the half light of the moon I could at least see the path ahead of me, and the strange bouncing light seemed to have stopped on the path to wait for my arrival. Walking more quickly now, I called out again, "Who are you? Is that you, Stokes?"

I walked deeper into the twisting garden, to the left and then to the right again until I felt disoriented.

What was I doing? This was none of my business, was it? This was not my house or my property. I was only a visitor here. Who did I think I was, policing the grounds as if I were a true Cottonwood? I had no weapon or any other way to defend myself, but I wasn't thinking clearly as I pushed toward the light that now began to pulsate. The amber color darkened, and suddenly the light disappeared. I scrambled down the hedge, scratching myself on a thorny branch. I swore under my breath—it was a word I had never used before, but I had heard Maundy use it plenty of times. Yet I did not stop. I could not explain this compulsion, but I had to find and identify the source of the light. I stepped out of the maze into a clearing and nearly fell over dead.

Standing in the center circle of the maze was a man, a tall man wearing a fine suit with white collars and no hat. Unmoving, he watched me as I approached just as if he were a statue. I had passed many statues in this garden on my journey here, but none were as frightening as the man who stood before me. I paused about twenty feet from him, waiting for some indication that he was a living being. Another breeze blew through the Moonlight Garden, and on the breeze I smelled magnolias, burning leaves and something else...

My hands flew into fists, and I looked around to see if anyone else had joined us. If there were two men I should certainly run, but I saw no one else. What should I do? Should I turn to flee the garden? I stared in disbelief as a whirlwind of leaves blew between us, blasting my gown and hair. In seconds, it had lashed my hair completely free from its pins. As the wind blew past me I could plainly see that the intruder's hair did not move! He was certainly a statue—or something. A feeling of dread filled my soul with horror, and finally I gained control of my legs. As quickly as I had run into the garden, I began to run out.

I took a right turn down the long hedgerow and ran left, traveling under the blooming dogwoods. I took another left and ran the length of the magnolia-lined trail. My eyes were wide, and my breath came fast and hard. I knew I was heading the right way—there were pods and leaves covering the ground, and the white petals shone bright in the moonlight. My forgotten torn hem caught my foot, and I tripped and went sliding across a pile of damp, musky leaves. I skinned my elbow, but I could not really feel the pain.

I heard footsteps behind me on the leaves and knew I was not alone. I was too afraid to move.

Maybe if I remain very still, he will not see me!

Slowly I pushed my hair out of my face and could see a pair of shoes a few feet from me. With complete horror, I looked up…and there he was, glaring down at me. The stranger reached his hand toward me, and his long nails were dirty and gray. I scrambled away from him, scooting back on my hands and climbing awkwardly to my feet. I stood breathing hard as the thing surveyed me. Since I stood frozen, afraid for my life, I stared back. His unearthly pale skin appeared as if it had never seen the sun. He had a thin, narrow nose, sculpted lips and dark eyes—eyes that had no life in them. On closer inspection I could see that his jacket and trousers were dusty as if he slept in the dirt. My soul was offended on such a deep level, but I could barely understand it. Then it occurred to me. This man was not alive—I was looking into the face of a ghost.

As the awareness of my situation dawned upon me, I could see the amusement in his eyes. I knew who he was—or at least *what* he was, and he knew that too. Since he was not leaving or moving I asked him, "What are you doing here?"

He took a step toward me, and instinctively I moved backwards. In an elegant dead voice he said, "I am waiting for someone."

"Who are you waiting for?" I whispered in the darkness. He moved toward me without moving his feet. It was a sort of glide. He was only a few feet from me now, and as I watched his face began to change...the skin became pinker, the dark eyes took on a dark blue color, and he appeared to breathe. The breeze blew again, lifting the hair off of his collar. Despite the amazing effect, I knew it was all an illusion. He wanted me to think he was alive, but I knew he was not. A smile curled on his lips, and I could see his perfect white teeth.

"It does not matter now, Delilah. She is not here, but you will do. Would you like to take a walk with me?" He offered his hand to me as innocently as a child, but I had no intention of reaching for it.

"No, I don't think I will." There we stood facing one another, he unmoving and my feet locked in place. Then I heard a voice, a familiar voice, a living voice calling to me from the house.

"Delilah? Come inside! There is a storm brewing." The garden intruder glanced at the doorway and then at me. He smiled and rudely licked his lips before he disappeared, melting away until his image vanished. Finally free to move, I bolted toward the door, remembering to lift my tattered hem as I ran. I climbed the steps and scurried through the open door and into the arms of my cousin.

"Delilah! Look at you! What happened? You are as cold as ice. Come inside now and I'll make you a hot cup of tea." I wept on her shoulder and clung to her as if she were the only thing that could save me from death. "Docie! Come quickly!"

Kara's servant walked serenely into the hallway, her hands clasped before her. "Yes? What is it?" The older woman was wearing a long flannel nightgown, and her gray hair hung in a long braid over her shoulder.

"My cousin has seen something that frightened her. Have Stokes search the garden, and please bring us a cup of tea. Quickly now!" Karah led me away, her arm about my waist. I glanced over my shoulder at Docie. The woman had not moved. In fact, she stood in the hallway watching us with a smile on her face.

She knew exactly what I had seen in the garden, and she wasn't surprised by it.

Chapter Thirteen—Carrie Jo

Before I left the house, I checked my email and was delighted to see that Desmond Taylor had replied with his answer: the Idlewood project was a go! I had done it—no, our team had done it! I felt excited by the prospect of beginning a new project. It would take a lot of time, probably a few years, but it would be worth it if we could stop the house from rotting into the Mobile landscape and return Idlewood to its proper place in society.

Ashland had left early for a meeting with his attorney about some mysterious project. I wasn't too sure about this new attorney. She seemed very hands-on, but she was a friend of his from high school; working with him would kind of be her big break. I trusted Ashland. He had been unfaithful to me only subconsciously. I had no reason to believe that there was anything funny going on, but my gut still told me to keep an eye on her.

Rachel greeted me and pointed to the coffeepot. "Made some fresh. Get it while it's hot."

Just the idea of drinking coffee made me queasy, and she must've seen the expression on my face. "What? I thought you loved my coffee."

My hand flew to my stomach, and I nodded glumly. "I do love your coffee, but my child? Not so much."

"Oh my God! Are you serious?" Rachel ran around her desk and put her arms around me. "I'm so happy! I'm going to be Aunt Rachel! When is he due? Or she due? Do we know what we're having?"

I laughed at her excitement. It felt good to tell my secret. "Not yet, but I'm sure we will find out soon enough. I have another appointment in a couple of weeks. Maybe by then they can do the ultrasound and we can see something."

She hugged me again, and before I could get to my office the front door opened. A very happy-looking Henri and Detra Ann walked in. "Hey, guys." I greeted them with a smile.

"Is this how you always start your workday, with a group hug?" Detra Ann laughed and hugged me too.

Before I could say anything, Rachel blurted out, "It's so wonderful! Carrie Jo is going to have a baby."

"I heard! I'm so happy for y'all!" Detra Ann hugged me again.

Henri put his arm around me. "I had to tell her. You and Ashland will make wonderful parents. Congratulations again, CJ."

"Thank you. It is pretty wonderful. So what brings you two by? Not that I'm not glad to see you for any reason."

"Actually I came to talk to you about Lenore."

Thinking that Henri would want privacy I said, "Let's go to my office. Rachel made some wonderful coffee if you'd like some."

"I think we're good."

I sat behind my desk and invited them to take the two seats in front of me. I tossed my purse in the bottom drawer and turned my attention to my friends. "You should know she's gone. I mean, she left this morning before Ashland or I got up. She mentioned something yesterday about getting a job as a housekeeper. I didn't ask Doreen this morning, but I think she plans on talking to her."

Detra Ann leaned back in her chair and glanced at Henri. He said, "Lenore has always walked to the beat of a different drummer, even before Aleezabeth disappeared, but her behavior has gotten worse since. I am grateful that you allowed her to spend the night with you, but that is not a solution. I cannot put you guys in the middle of her mess, especially with a baby coming. I am not sure what she's capable of."

"I agree that Lenore is…quirky. But I'm not sure she's dangerous. Then again, you know her better than I do."

"I think I have a way to help her. What if, somehow, we could find out what happened to Aleezabeth? I mean, I would never ask for myself, but…she needs to know or she is never going to move past it. That's why I am here, Carrie Jo. I know you and Ashland both have skills in this area. What if we could solve the mystery, find my cousin and bring her home? I think that would…" Just then, my phone rang. Despite my attempts to ignore it, Rachel poked her head in the doorway.

"I hate to interrupt, but that's Desmond Taylor on the phone. He's on a cruise. I'm not sure when you could call him back. Do you want to speak with him?"

I didn't know what to say to Henri. Was he asking me to dream about Aleezabeth? "Forgive me, y'all, but I have to take this. Just give me a second."

"We can talk later." Henri stood, and Detra Ann just stared at him.

"It's not that you guys aren't important to me. It's just that—"

Henri raised his hand and gave me a dismissive wave. "I should never have asked." He walked out of the office; I could hear the front door chimes, and I sat staring open-mouthed at Detra Ann.

"What did I do?"

"Don't worry about him. He's just worried about Lenore. And no matter what he tells you, he's not over what happened to Aleezabeth. Tell you what—why don't we meet you for dinner and then we can talk."

"That sounds great. Why don't you guys come over about six? I'm really sorry, Detra Ann."

"Nothing to worry about. You leave him to me. We will be there." She walked out of my office in her shiny taupe heels.

"Okay!" I called after her, still puzzled by what just happened. I picked up the phone.

Desmond Taylor might have been on a cruise, but he was certainly in work mode. He had a slew of questions, and I did my best to answer them. After the thirty-minute call ended, I couldn't help but worry about

Henri. It was not like him to be short-tempered with me—I knew something was seriously wrong.

The day dragged by, but finally five o'clock came around and I waved goodbye to Rachel as I headed home. Doreen had graciously agreed to cook for our dinner guests, and my stomach was grumbling. I found Ashland in my office using my computer. I dumped my purse and briefcase on the side table, slid my arms around his neck and kissed the top of his head.

"Whatcha doing?"

"Just checking on a few things. You know, I never did give you *my* anniversary present." He turned the wooden chair around and patted his leg playfully.

"You're right." I slid into his lap and wrapped my arms around his neck. "But unfortunately your gift is going to have to wait. We have dinner guests coming, remember? I texted you earlier."

He smiled wickedly and said, "This will only take a minute."

I blushed and scolded him, "Ashland."

"It's not that, and I'm pretty sure that those kinds of *gifts* take a little more than a minute." I smiled back at him and punched him playfully on the arm. "Open the browser," he said.

"What?"

"Open the browser on the computer. I want you to see this."

I reached over and pulled up the browser window he had minimized. It was a website featuring historic Mobile landmarks. I had to admit that I was puzzled. "Okay, so this is Widow's Row. I have seen this before. What am I looking for?"

"Tell me about it."

"This house was originally part of Widow's Row. It was housing for Civil War widows—there were quite a few of them. But there was something of a scandal there around the turn of the century. At the end of this street would have been the Southern Market. Right here." I pointed to a map that showed the layout of the old city. "One row of houses ran east, and the second ran west, that way. Of course, the county courthouse was across the street back then. It's a shame that most of those houses are gone."

"Not all of them are."

"Really?"

"A few have been wonderfully restored, like the Murray House, but there is one that's kind of been left behind. It's on Eslava Street."

"Eslava…it runs parallel to Virginia Street, right?"

"Yes."

"So what am I looking for?"

He reached around me and clicked on another screen. A tiny house, sometimes called a "shotgun" house, popped up on the screen. "It's yours. I thought it would make the perfect office for your new business. You could restore it and really show off your talents. And of course, you'd be restoring a patch of Mobile. What do you think?"

Tears welled up in my eyes. "I think it's wonderful." I put my arms around his neck again and hugged him. "I love you."

"I love you too."

"And I didn't get you anything."

"Nonsense. You gave me the best gift of all." He nervously touched my stomach. I nodded and put my hand over his. I kissed him, feeling so grateful not only for the wonderful gift but for the fact that I had someone as wonderful as Ashland in my life. What a fool I had been to make such a big deal out of his stupid dreams! I felt blessed beyond belief.

I heard voices in the hall. "Oops. To be continued. Our guests have arrived a few minutes early."

With one last kiss I scooted out of his lap, and together we walked out of the office holding hands like two teenagers.

"Hey, guys!" I called to them. "Glad you could make it. I'll check with Doreen on dinner. Be right back." Ashland squeezed my hand, and I went to see if I could help in the kitchen. As expected Doreen was a whirlwind of activity; a sauce pot on the stove filled the kitchen with delicious flavor. She slid the pork roast out of the oven and set the pan on the stove top before she spun around and gasped.

"Mrs. Stuart! You almost gave me a heart attack." She pushed her eyeglasses back to the bridge of her nose and gave me a goodhearted yet disapproving scowl.

"Sorry," I said sincerely. "Thank you for going the extra mile tonight, Doreen. Smells delicious." I stuck a spoon in the sauce before she could object. "Can I do anything?" The sauce was delicious. Not like Bette would have made, but I couldn't wait to dig in.

"No, ma'am. I have this under control. Dinner should be ready in about twenty minutes. I think your guests are a bit early."

"Yes they are, and we aren't in a big rush," I said as I stole a warm yeast roll from the covered basket on the bar.

"You never said if you wanted me to serve. Did you want this buffet style?"

"Buffet style is perfect. We can wait on ourselves." I resisted the urge to hug her. Doreen didn't enjoy being touched—or surprised. I seemed to always do both. Leaving dinner in good hands, I went to join my friends, but Detra Ann caught me in the hallway and waved me into the bathroom. I giggled as she closed the door behind us.

"What's going on? Are you dying to tell me the details?" I asked teasingly. Her distressed look made me change my tone immediately. "Detra Ann?"

"I thought about calling you after we left this morning, but I didn't know what to say."

"You should have. I'm sorry about that phone call."

"You must think I'm a horrible person. I mean, I never meant for this to happen with Henri. It just sort of happened."

I grinned at her. "What? You must be the only person who didn't see this coming. And of course I don't think you're horrible—this is the way it should be. Nobody expects you to mourn forever, Detra Ann. This isn't the 1800s."

Sitting on the side of the tub with her head in her hands, she whispered, "I just don't know. I don't know if this is right. I don't know if this is what I want. That's horrible to say, isn't it?"

I sat on the floor next to her and waited for her to look at me. Sitting this close, I could see the dark circles under her eyes that she tried to hide with expensive concealer. She hadn't been sleeping and was much thinner than she had been last year. She didn't have any extra weight to begin with. "I think it's time for you to think about yourself. Not your mom. Not Henri. Yourself. It's okay to take care of you. And if you're not sure how you feel about him, then slow down. No one will fault you for that."

"I'm leaving, Carrie Jo. I took a job in Atlanta."

"Oh wow."

"He thinks last night changed everything, but it didn't. He doesn't understand what I've been through. I mean, I know he knows—I've talked about it plenty of times—but he doesn't know how I feel. It's just too soon. It's too much. I just can't. And there's this other thing."

"What?"

"Lenore is right. I am a shade, a ghost. I think I am marked. I think—no, I know—that something bad is going to happen to me."

Instinctively I grabbed her hands and said, "No! Don't listen to her. She doesn't know what she's talking about. We beat those ghosts, and it's over. End of subject. Lenore is crazy—I caught her talking on the phone to nobody last night. There was no one on the other end." No way was I telling Detra Ann what Lenore said or what Ashland saw.

Her beautiful eyes widened, but she continued, "You and I both know that with that house it's never truly over. I can't pretend that I understand why all of this happened. I still don't know why Bette had to go and why Terrence is gone. What was the connection—what made me so special that I escaped? It's not fair, and I think I just got lucky. But my luck is wearing out. If I don't leave, if I don't make a run for it, well, then I'm going to join them. I hear things. I see things. Dark things. If I sit still for too long shadows creep in. I can't even close my eyes for very long. Something is coming for me, CJ."

I heard Ashland call me from the hallway, and I scrambled to my feet and opened the door. "Right here. Be there in just a second." I didn't offer any explanation other than that. He'd have to wait. I closed the door and sat next to Detra Ann.

"Listen to me. If you decide to leave, that's fine if that's what you need to do. But if you're leaving just to run away from some phantom, then you should stay. We can fight this, Detra Ann, and we *can* do it if we stick together. That was the mistake I made the last time. I took off half-cocked into that hospital room, and look where it got us. Bette is gone." A sob escaped my throat. "And that's on me. TD's gone. And that's on me. They had no idea what I was doing, and I put them in a horrible situation. You are not alone, and I'm not going to let you fight this by yourself. Let's go in there right now, tell them what's going on and get everyone on board so we can come up with some sort of plan. Enough with working behind the scenes—we need to be honest and put everything out in the open."

"I can't do that to Henri. He is so broken up about Aleezabeth and Lenore. I don't think he can handle one more thing right now. And let me remind you that you have a baby to think about. I can't have you fighting Death on my behalf. I won't do it. I just wanted you to know that I value your friendship. I am glad I got to know you."

"Me too, but don't talk like I'll never see you again."

"I want you to promise me something." I didn't like the sound of this, but I nodded. "Promise me that you will look after Ashland. If anything were to ever happen to me and you ditch him, I will come back and haunt you."

"Of course I will. But don't talk like this. We're sticking together, remember?" Before she could protest, there was a knock on the door.

"What's going on in there? Carrie Jo are you okay?" When did Ashland get to be so nosy?

"Yes. I was just feeling a little sick. I'm okay now. Coming right out." Detra Ann and I hugged, and I emerged from the bathroom with my hand over my stomach. "Must be evening sickness."

Soon the four of us were chatting, but it was impossible to really have a conversation with Doreen coming in and out. She insisted on waiting on us even though we'd agreed on a more informal buffet style. Thirty minutes later, she waved goodbye, and I gathered the supper plates and quickly carried them to the kitchen. I'd tidy those up later, but I had something to do. No way was I going to lose another friend. I decided it was time to take charge. I meant what I'd said about no more secrets. Wiping my hands on the kitchen towel, I marched back into the living room and stood with my hands on my hips. I didn't give a hoot about what they were talking about. I spilled my guts.

"Detra Ann needs our help, y'all. I know that you have something to say, Henri, and I am sorry about this morning's interruption. But this is a situation that can't wait."

Detra Ann scowled at me. "Carrie Jo…stop."

"Nope. You might be mad at me forever, but at least you'll be alive. We have to tell them. So tell them already!" Ashland and Henri stared at me like I had two heads. "I'm not kidding. You tell them or I will."

Detra Ann shot to her feet and glared at me. "I didn't want you to say anything, CJ!"

"Well, I did, and I refuse to lose another friend! You can hate me later, but tell them what's going on."

She slid her hands into the pockets of her fitted sweatshirt and paced the carpet in front of the big window on the side of the house. The streetlight was on out front, but the side of the house looked dark and gloomy. After a few moments, she leaned against the windowsill and stared out into the darkness with her back to us. "Lenore is right. Something is following me. I knew it the day I left the hospital. At first I thought it was the pain medicine. God, that stuff is awful. That's why I prefer drinking. Booze doesn't make my skin crawl or cause me to hallucinate. Pain medication makes me loopy big time, but that wasn't it. At first it only happened once, maybe twice, a day. I was walking down the sidewalk in front of my mother's house on Palladium Drive, and I passed that big oak that stretches almost into the street. You know the one, Ashland, the one we used to climb. As soon as I stepped into the shadow, I heard it groan, like it wanted to devour me." She shivered, turned around and leaned with her back against the window, her hands still in her pockets. "By the time I got into Mom's house I was shaking so bad I thought I would pass out." She began pacing again.

"Then the shadows in my house began to groan whenever I came close to them. You can't know what it's like having to leave the lights on 24/7 like you're a four-year old! I don't dare turn a light off because the shadows don't just groan now—they call my name!" Detra Ann's voice rose in fear. Henri reached for her, but she raised her hand and shook her head. "No. Let me finish." She took a deep breath and continued, "A month after the hospital event, I was in the shower when the light went out in my bathroom. The bulb blew—that's what I told myself anyway. There I was in the shower, naked and soaking wet, just waiting to die. The groans grew louder and louder—I could feel the darkness gathering. I tripped out of the shower and crawled to the bathroom door. A slimy hand grabbed my foot and pulled me back, but I kept struggling to get away. Finally I remembered the Lord's Prayer. I said it, like you did the other night, Ashland. I said it, and it let me go. I reached the door handle and turned it, and I was free. Then I called Henri to change the light bulb for me." She reached out and squeezed his hand. "You have been so good to me. I don't deserve you."

Henri's dark eyes sparkled with tears. "Don't say that. I am the lucky one. I love you, Detra Ann."

"I know," she said sadly. She turned back to the big window. Nobody said a word; I sure didn't know what to say. "Even now, if I stepped into the yard and stood under that tree where the shadows are the darkest, it would take me and I would never escape." She peered out the blinds, and my skin began to crawl.

"Detra Ann, get away from the window," Ashland warned her sternly. He stood in front of me and waved his hand behind him, and I got off the couch and moved to the doorway. I couldn't see anything, but apparently my husband did.

It didn't seem to faze her. "See? I can see the darkness gathering now. It's just waiting for me. I don't know what's in those shadows, but I know if it touches me,

I'll die. Tell me I'm wrong! Any of you! Tell me I'm wrong!"

"Detra Ann, get away from the window!"

Tearing her eyes away from the darkness, she looked at Ashland. As she did, the window behind her shattered with a loud boom, and pieces of glass flew across the living room. Ashland fell on top of me to protect me, and Henri snatched Detra Ann's hand and pulled her to the ground. As we lay there trying to figure out who was hurt and what happened, the chandelier flickered.

"Everyone get up now!" Ashland yelled. "Upstairs, everyone!"

We did as we were told and climbed the stairs like four maniacs. I flipped on light switches as we ran so none of the shadows could touch Detra Ann. She wasn't crying or saying anything at all, just running with fear in her eyes. I couldn't blame her. If Death were chasing me and using shadows to reach me, I would be fearful too. When we made it to the end of the hallway, I grabbed her hands. "Don't run away from us, Detra Ann. Stay close, okay?" She bobbled her blond head. Her makeup was running under her eyes, and her hands shook.

Standing on tiptoe, I tried to see the ground floor, but it was completely dark. I imagined that I too could almost hear an inaudible whisper.

"Oh God, it's calling my name. Lenore was right! It is Death. He wants me! I cheated him, and now he wants me. He's come to claim me!"

"Well, he's going to have to fight us if he wants you because he isn't going to take you, Detra Ann! We're safe here. There is light up here, see?" I heard the light bulb pop above us, and the light faded.

"Oh my God!" she shouted and ran into the guest room.

"Stop, Detra Ann! Wait for me!" I ran to her, flipping on every light I could as I went. "Follow me. I have a flashlight somewhere in my bedroom." Grabbing her hand I called, "Ashland! Where is the flashlight?" Coming to himself now, he ran to us and opened the closet. Hidden in the back was a huge Maglite that could light up the neighborhood when fully charged. He turned it on. The light was so bright it was nearly blinding. Henri was holding Detra Ann now, and she was weeping.

"I love you. I love you. I love you," she repeated over and over again.

"Shh…it's okay. Shh, now. It's okay. We are all here together."

Then the guest room lights went out and the lamps popped. We were in total darkness except for the Maglite, which lit up the entire room with harsh white light. So far it wasn't flickering, but who knew how long it would last? We heard a sound, a slapping, crashing sound. The tree limbs from the oaks that surrounded our house were slapping the windows—slapping them so hard they were all breaking! Between the crashing and the groaning, it was a horrible cacophony. Surely the neighbors would hear this! Somebody would come help us! But what if they didn't?

"I love you, Henri. I'm sorry. I am sorry..." Detra Ann was crying quietly now. The whispers became louder and more threatening. Henri held her as if it might be his last chance. Tears ran down his cheeks.

"Ashland," I said fearfully as he wrapped his arms around me.

Suddenly the smashing and crashing of the branches ceased, and the door to the bedroom flew open—a tall figure stood in the doorway. We gasped and waited. A tall figure stepped out of the darkness and into the brightness of the Maglite.

I couldn't believe it—it was Lenore!

Chapter Fourteen—Detra Ann

"You believe me now, don't you? I said you were a shade." She spat the words out like she hated me. Like I wanted to be in this battle with Death itself.

"How did you get up here? Is there a way out?" I demanded, suddenly feeling hopeful.

"The only way out is the way you came in, and it's pitch black outside." She leaned against the doorframe staring at me.

Carrie Jo stood by me protectively. "How did you get up here? Did you see it?"

"I saw nothing but the wind blowing and the house dark. I can feel it, though. It's still very close."

"She's right. We're not out of the woods yet," Ashland added.

"I don't understand why this is happening! Why won't it leave me alone? How do I make it stop? Do you know, or are you going to continue to hate me? Why don't you try to help me since you seem to know so much?" Anger and frustration rose up inside me. She could help me, I knew it, but for some reason she wouldn't. "Why? What have I ever done to you? I don't even know you, Lenore!"

She didn't answer but glared at me with her almond-shaped eyes. Her mouth was a pair of hard lines.

"I know who can help us," Carrie Jo said in a rush.

"Who?"

"Father Portier! He'll know how we can defeat Death."

"What makes you so sure, Carrie Jo?" Henri asked.

"Because he's already dead."

"What?"

"There's no time to talk about this." She waved the flashlight and walked out the door. "Let's go before this thing comes back." She grabbed my hand, and we scrambled down the stairs with lightning speed, the guys following behind us. CJ grabbed her purse off the entryway table, and we headed out the door. We climbed into her BMW, and I was surprised to see Lenore climb in the backseat beside me. CJ slid the key into the ignition and we rolled down the driveway onto the crowded street. Ashland passed me the flashlight, and I held it like my life depended on it. Maybe it did.

"Oh no, it's a parade night," Carrie Jo said as we drove down Dauphin and nearly ran into a barricade. "We'll have to go around to Conte Street. Maybe that's not blocked off." She turned right and eased down the street slowly. There were people everywhere.

"Where exactly are we headed?" Ashland asked her in a worried voice. "Not to Seven Sisters, I hope."

"No, I don't think this has to do with the house. Not directly, anyway. We're going to the cemetery. That's where the gate is, and that is where I met the priest. This must be why. I didn't put it together until tonight."

"Hold on now. Nobody said anything about a cemetery. We're trying to escape Death, not knock on his door," Lenore said fearfully.

"As you said, he's not looking for you, right? Then you have nothing to fear." Henri snarled at her impatiently. "And nobody asked you to come."

"Someone has to look out for you, Henri Devecheaux." He snorted and looked out the window.

"What are you thinking? How are these things connected?" Ashland asked, his blue eyes full of questions.

"Detra Ann is a spiritual person. She said that she was able to escape it when it came for her in the bathroom by praying the Lord's Prayer."

"Okay…"

"There must be some prayer we can use to make it leave her alone for good. The priest told me to look for the secret."

Ashland's face was filled with doubt, but I piped in, "Listen, it might be a long shot, but I'm willing to go on a little faith here. Even if it means walking through a cemetery."

"What if the gate won't open? What if we can't get to the priest? You said yourself you don't know how you got there."

"It will open. It has to."

Ashland looked at me in the rearview mirror. "You sure you want to do this?"

I nodded, and Henri squeezed my hand. "I'll be right with you the whole time," he murmured.

Ashland nodded and said, "We'll have to park and walk. This is about as close as you're going to get." Carrie Jo pulled the car to the side of the road, claiming the last parking spot on the street. The sidewalks were jammed with revelers streaming toward the parade route. "Let's see. If we cut through that vacant lot, we should come out on Virginia Street, but the cemetery will still be a few blocks away. Keep the flashlight close and stay close to the group, Detra Ann."

"Got it," I replied. Ashland had nothing to worry about. I was never letting go of Henri's hand. "Let's go!" We emptied the car and walked down the sidewalk away from the gathering partiers. I suddenly wished I'd grabbed my jacket before we left. My sweatshirt provided little protection from the frigid night air. My heart hammered in my chest as I scanned the sidewalks for shadows. There were plenty.

"Go ahead and turn on your flashlight. Just point it down at the ground. We don't want to attract attention," Henri whispered to me. With cold, stiff fingers, I slid the button into the on position and breathed a sigh of relief as the shadows around me vanished. Lenore slipped her arm through mine—I didn't pull away, but I clutched Henri's hand tighter. In the distance a marching band blasted "On Broadway" to the appreciation of the happy parade watchers—the sound echoed through the narrow streets of downtown Mobile. I could hear the occasional blast of police sirens. In a strange way it comforted me knowing that the police were so close. As if they could actually help me.

Ashland paused on the sidewalk. "We're getting closer. How are you doing?"

"So far, so good," I stammered. The cold made my teeth chatter. Lenore's fingers were about to freeze me to death. Of all of us, she was the least prepared for the cold weather. She wore thin tights and an oversize, long-sleeved t-shirt. Henri was the only one who'd had the good sense to dress warmly, but then again none of us expected to be visiting a graveyard at night. I waved the flashlight on the grass in front of me and carefully stepped only in the light. For some reason, I thought about TD. I hadn't thought about him as much lately, but the love I had for him had not diminished at all. Some girls had high school sweethearts, and others had college sweethearts. I had neither of those. TD had been it for me, or at least I thought so until he disappeared. In the months following his death, I had a difficult time sorting through my feelings. TD had left me for a ghost. I had been pushed unwillingly into a battle and fought for my life, and all for what? I felt abandoned. Life was completely unfair. I was reminded of one of my favorite quotes from an English literature class. "Life makes fools of us all."

So why was I thinking of TD now?

"This way, here's the street," a Mardi Gras vendor shouted at us. An inflatable fleur-de-lis hat perched upon his head, and his cart was full of parade swag. Before he could begin his spiel, Ashland raised his hand politely and said, "Sorry. Not today." We left the man staring after us as we shuffled down the street. The parade was a few streets over, so there was nobody else on Virginia Street.

I looked over my shoulder and said to no one in particular, "I wonder why he's over here." To my surprise, the man and his cart had disappeared.

"Don't pay any attention to that. He's just having fun with you. Keep that light on and keep walking." Lenore's furious whisper made my heart pound. I knew exactly who she was talking about. I did as she instructed and kept my eyes on the ground, always stepping only in the light.

"There it is!" The Magnolia Cemetery sign swung gently in the breeze. The gate stood open—it was a foreboding sign, as if someone had expected us to visit.

Carrie Jo paused before we walked inside the graveyard. "There are no lights in here, so you'll have to lead the way. Just walk straight toward the back; that's the gate were looking for. Are you going to be okay?"

I swallowed hard. "Oh God, I hope so." Our little group shuffled together down the narrow walkway. I had been here once before in middle school, but that was a long time ago. I certainly wasn't an expert on navigating this massive maze of graves. Immediately to the right I noticed a row of mausoleums. Even though there was very little moonlight, they seemed to have an eerie glow about them.

Lenore shook her head. "I ain't going in there. Too many ghosts. I'll meet y'all on the other side." Before we could argue with her, she was already halfway down the sidewalk.

I chewed my lip as I watched her disappear down the street. I wanted a shot of whiskey, but it was too late for liquid courage. "Carrie Jo, I've been thinking. What if the gate doesn't work? What if only you can go through it? What if it takes us somewhere else?"

"We connected the last time, remember? I think we can do it again. What choice do we have?" She looked so hopeful, but I felt anything but confident. The last time we went "ghost busting," I ended up the prisoner of a murderous spirit who was convinced that I was his dead wife. The wife he hung from a chandelier until she died. Now CJ wanted to go see another ghost. But she was right...what choice did I have?

"Alright. Then let's do this. Wait." I reached for Henri and kissed him on the lips. "Just to remind myself that I'm alive." I smiled up into his worried brown eyes. "It's okay, right?"

He said, "I plan on keeping you alive. I want a second date." Despite the situation, I couldn't help but love him for saying that. I waved the light around nervously, took a deep breath and entered the cemetery. Some of the newest tombstones were located near the entrance. I remembered seeing these on that middle school trip when we came to take rubbings of the tombstones. I didn't like cemeteries even as a child. I'd found the first suitable grave there was, made my rubbing and waited impatiently for everyone to finish theirs. A few feet into the graveyard, a shell pathway began. It glowed in the dim light. I waved the flashlight around again and gasped. Something ran from the light—it looked like a cat. At least I hoped it was a cat. My eyes couldn't stop flitting about searching for anything that moved.

"How far is it, CJ?"

"All the way in the back." The four of us hurried down the pathway together, Henri and I in front, Carrie Jo and Ash right behind us.

Ashland cleared his throat. "Guys, I don't know whether to tell you this or not, but…"

I spun around, waving my flashlight furiously.

"You're going to blind us, Detra Ann," he complained.

"Sorry. What is it?"

"Lenore was right—this place is teeming with ghosts. And they don't look too happy to see us here."

Carrie Jo asked, "Anyone we know?"

He paused and looked into the darkness. "Not that I can tell, but the shadows are moving now. Just like before…when whatever it was appeared at the house."

"Death. It's Death, Ashland. Just say it."

"We don't have time for this, and we can't stop…go now! Run!" He didn't have to tell me twice. I took off running toward the distant gate. Carrie Jo was beside me. I paused for a second when a looming figure appeared on the right of the path. It was a massive angel statue with his arms stretched to the heavens. "Oh Lord!" I whispered and kept running. The light from my Maglite bounced as I ran, and I could hear the whispers collecting around me. Ashland was right. The shadows were gathering, and now there were many ghosts to contend with. In my mind I could see them reaching for me, demanding that I return to their realm to take my proper place among those who had surrendered life.

No! It's not my time!

My chest burned—it had been a long time since I had gone for a run. I was so out of shape, but adrenaline-fueled fear kicked in and propelled me forward ahead of my friends. I turned the corner of the path, and a gruesome-looking cherub sat perched on top of a moldy gravestone. Long ago, some grieving family member had thought the fat-faced figure would be a fitting tribute to their lost loved one. I couldn't disagree more. Ahead of me, I could see a looming shadow that covered the walkway. I waved the Maglite at it, but it didn't disappear. I came to a screeching halt, and my friends piled behind me. All of us were panting for breath.

"Oh my God!"

"Go around it!" Carrie Jo screamed at me.

Clumsily, I tripped up a small round hill, and the flashlight flew from my hand. Carrie Jo grabbed it and reached for my hand, pulling me to my feet. I heard a swishing sound and felt a disturbance in the air around me. Someone or something was there—I just couldn't see them.

"You can't stop! Believe me," Ashland yelled at me. My friends nearly picked me up off the ground and carried me to the back gate. I was almost in tears and not thinking at all.

"Come on, baby. Almost there," Henri said, looking over his shoulder as he cleared a small row of graves running behind me. It was the first time he'd ever called me baby. I liked it. I suddenly realized that I did love Henri. It was different from my love for TD, but it was love nonetheless.

CJ waved the flashlight at the back gate—only fifty feet away. "Almost there!" she shouted over the growing whispers. Suddenly a flash of light appeared in front of the gate. Then the light disappeared, leaving the figure behind. "Lenore?" she asked.

It wasn't Lenore. I knew that figure just like I knew my own. That was Terrence Dale. I snatched the light from Carrie Jo and shined it at the gate again. He didn't disappear. He stood staring at us, his face not unfriendly or reproachful. It was him! I heard Henri gasp beside me. "Is that…"

"TD…" I whispered, tears filling my eyes. He wasn't dead at all but completely alive. There was even a halo of light around him. Had we gotten it wrong somehow—was he alive but stuck in the past? Maybe he needed our help to break free from wherever he was stuck. I couldn't think straight, and I was freezing. I could see my breath now in the light. He looked directly at me and gave me a heartbreaking smile. Then he vanished.

"No!" I yelled and ran toward the gate. "Terrence!"

Chapter Fifteen—Carrie Jo

Before I could stop her, Detra Ann flew through the gate and disappeared, taking the flashlight with her. The three of us stood in the dark cemetery and stared at the gaping entrance. "She's gone," Henri said. "I was supposed to protect her, and now she's gone." He banged on the gate and walked in circles, his hands on his head. He let out an anguished cry. "Do something! Where is she?"

"She passed through the gate, Henri. She didn't wait for us. She was supposed to wait." I didn't know what else to say. I needed a moment to think.

"What are we supposed to do now?"

"Henri!" A voice called out from the darkness of the adjoining street. Lenore appeared on the other side of the gate. "Where is she?"

"She's gone."

"I was afraid of this." Lenore tapped her lip with her finger. "Well, time for plan B. Do we have one?" Everyone stared at me.

I paced in front of the gate. No, we didn't. My half-cocked plan A was all I had, and now Detra Ann was gone.

"Ashland, what do you see? Are the ghosts still here?"

He peered into the inky blackness and said, "No. They are all gone. There were dozens of them here just a minute ago."

"Shoot! When she ran through the gate, it must have closed the connection."

"How do you know that?" Lenore asked me suspiciously. "You done this before?"

"Kind of. We went through the wall together at the hospital. And when I walked through the gate the other night, I ended up in the basilica. Look, we all saw her. The gate was open, and now it's not and all the activity stopped. That's got to mean something, doesn't it?"

"She's gone." Henri sat on the ground and stared into the darkness.

"We're not giving up. We have to go to the church. Maybe the gate works both ways."

"Sounds like plan B to me. Let's go. I'm freezing."

I walked through the open gate, closed my eyes and half hoped it would work, but nothing happened. Ashland looked glum, Henri wasn't talking at all, and Lenore acted like this was all a joke. As we walked toward the church, the music got louder. We would have to cross the parade route to get to St. Joseph Street. The Order of Polka Dots sailed down the street on vibrant floats, while the crowds roared, pleading for beads, moon pies and candy.

"Carrie Jo? You okay?" Lenore stood inches from my face. "Hey!"

"Yeah, I'm okay." I suddenly realized how lovely Lenore could be if she actually cared about what she looked like. She grabbed my hand and dragged me behind her as we dashed across the street.

"Lenore! Wait! You're hurting me." I snatched my hand away.

She walked toward me and got in my face again. "You don't have time. Death has her, and he ain't gonna wait," she shouted at me over the music. I waved to Ashland and Henri, who were stuck on the other side of the street. A police officer on horseback stepped into my line of sight so I couldn't see them anymore. "Carrie Jo, listen to me. Don't get them involved, please. Trust me when I tell you that it can only be bad. We can do this together. Let's go. They know where we are going, and they'll catch up." A drunken reveler pushed me as he chased after a float. Another one brushed up against me and leered at me. One thing was for sure—we couldn't stand here on the street. Maybe Lenore was right. Could I really put Ashland and Henri in danger? I'd already managed to lose Detra Ann. I looked one more time toward the street, but the crowd was growing and people were pushing and shoving.

"Let's go," I shouted back at her and began following her through the crowd toward St. Joseph and Clairborne Streets. People with painted faces and novelty lighted headbands circled me and shouted, "Happy Mardi Gras!" A man in the parade spun me about playfully as I struggled against him, feeling a surge of panic. Finally I broke free from the crowd and pushed to the edge where I could see the red and white building of the cathedral in the distance. Lenore took my hand, and together we ran as fast as we could. I glanced behind me, half hoping I would see Ashland

and Henri close, but they were nowhere to be found. We ran to the cast-iron gates, and I held on to the cold metal as I tried to catch my breath. I could plainly see that the gates and the church doors had been locked. I swore under my breath. Grabbing my hand again, Lenore led me down the sidewalk.

"Give me just a second. I have to catch my breath."

"We're running out of time. This way." Lenore pulled me toward the back of the building. This was the side that faced St. Joseph Street. I'd never explored this area before.

"Maybe we should call someone and ask them to let us in." I knew that was a stupid suggestion, but I was out of ideas. I wasn't sure what I was going to do even if I could get inside.

"Look! We can get in that way!" There were some narrow concrete stairs that led down to the basement of the church. That was unusual in itself, as most buildings in Mobile didn't have cellars. Especially here in the downtown area, as close as it was to Mobile Bay. Yet here it was right in front of me. She tugged on the gate twice, but it would not budge.

I looked over my shoulder again, half expecting to see the red-haired caretaker come running toward me, but the streets were empty. "Let's do it together." Lenore nodded, and we shoved hard on the gate. To my surprise, it worked: the gate rattled open, and we walked down the stairs, closing the gate behind us. The rusty old latch cut my finger, but I managed to wriggle it back into place without locking it. Better to make it look closed so no one suspected anything.

What were the chances that the door would be unlocked? Lenore blew on her cold fingers and then turned the round knob. It opened with a click, and she smiled at me as if to say, "See, I told you this would work." We walked inside the church basement, and I was immediately assaulted by the musty smell. When was the last time anyone had aired this room out? Lenore was fiddling with a lighter she retrieved from somewhere. She flicked the flame and moved it around slowly so we could get our bearings. "Looks like a mission closet or something. Hey! There are some coats!" She walked a few feet away and began digging through a pile.

"We can't take those. They belong to the church, Lenore."

"Okay, you freeze to death, but I'm borrowing a coat."

Standing there shivering while she slid on a warm brown coat was more than I could bear. "Alright, if we're just borrowing them." I grabbed a long black trench with an insulated lining and slid it on. I immediately felt warmer. Seeing a pile of woolen hats, I grabbed one of those too. "Where is that lighter? We have to get upstairs."

Lenore flicked the lighter again, and together we searched for the door. We found it, but it was locked, and no amount of banging would open it.

"Shoot! There has to be another door." I felt along the dusty walls, and Lenore walked in the opposite direction doing the same.

"Hey!" she yelled. "I think I found something over here. Come help me." I ran to her, practically tripping over a box of books that someone had left on the floor. "It's in the floor. Look!" Next to the back wall was a small hatch in the floor with a metal chain attached to it. "Help me." Together we tugged on the chain, and the hatch opened. The smell of moldy earth rose up to greet us. Lenore cast the light around the entrance quickly, but there wasn't much to see beyond a set of dodgy-looking wooden stairs.

"I don't know. Should we be going down those things?"

"It's the only option we have, isn't it?" Without another word, she was climbing down the ladder. I heard the wood creak and complain under her weight, and she was smaller than me.

I heard a thud coming from the entrance of the cellar. It sounded like someone was coming toward us. I hurried down the ladder and reached into the darkness. "Lenore!"

She clicked the lighter, but it wouldn't work. "I'm here. Take my hand." I did, and she clicked again until the lighter released a small flame. "This way."

The historian in me couldn't help but pay attention to the wooden beam that ran along the top of the passageway, the dirty gas lamps that hung from the walls and the random items that I occasionally tripped over like a shovel and a small metal cart.

"What on earth is this place?" she asked as she waved furiously at a cobweb.

"I'd say an underground railroad." I squinted around us in the dim light.

"Are we going the right way?"

"Stop a minute, Lenore. Listen!"

She scowled at me but kept quiet for a few seconds. "What's that?"

I tugged at my coat, pulling it about me tighter. Straining to listen, I heard a voice. It had to be Detra Ann! "That's her! Move faster, Lenore!" We blindly ran until we reached a fork in the tunnel.

"Where now?" she shouted. We stood waiting to hear something.

"Help me! Someone!"

"This way! She's this way!" I took off to the right and stumbled over an unseen obstacle as I ran toward Detra Ann's voice. Shafts of light filtered through the grate above us. I stood under it, looking up into the church, when I heard another noise, a scratching, fluttering sound. "There! Grab that and we'll climb. Maybe push the grate."

"Better idea. Let's go up those stairs."

How had I missed those? We hurried up the curved stairwell and into the church. The only light was dim candlelight. I didn't know when it happened, but somehow we had passed through the "gate" because we were in the old church. The walls were as they had been during my supernatural trip, painted burgundy and gold. According to my online research, the renovations had completely changed the look of the cathedral. In modern times, the basilica had white walls with gold accents.

"Let her go! You have no place here! Leave now!" It was Father Portier, standing in front of the altar. Detra Ann's blond hair swirled around her, moving in an unearthly black cloud that seemed to want to swallow her. "Go, now!" The priest stood rigidly in defiance, but a blast of the black cloud sent him flying backwards into the wooden pews. Horror and dread filled me as I watched the old man collapse into a heap.

"Father Portier!" I yelled, running toward him with Lenore beside me.

At that moment, Detra Ann saw me and screamed, "Run, CJ!" The black cloud expanded, shrank and expanded again. Suddenly it broke into a hundred smaller clouds, and I heard the scratching, fluttering sound again. In the blink of an eye, the clouds became crows that flew straight toward us with deadly focus.

"Get down! Under the pews!" I screamed, dragging the priest to the floor and crawling under the benches. The crows flew above us, diving occasionally to peck and scratch at us. Lenore screamed in pain, and I looked back under the pew toward Detra Ann, who lay on the floor about twenty feet away. "Father Portier! Please! Help us!" I shook him again and again until he began to stir.

The old man turned his head toward me and pleaded, "You have to go. Before it's too late."

"I am not leaving without my friend."

"You have no choice, I am afraid. He will not release her." I peeked out from under the bench at the spinning vortex of birds that threatened us.

"I am not leaving Detra Ann!" My heart pounded in my chest as I crawled under the benches toward the front of the church, crying and praying as I went. When I finally made it to the front of the church, I reached my hand out from under the pew. Just then an angry bird with a sharp beak dipped down and scratched my skin savagely. Crying out in pain, Detra Ann spotted me and shook her head. The black cloud gathered around her thin frame, and a hundred screeches echoed angrily through the church.

Defiantly I slid out from under the wooden bench and stood in the aisle. Lenore and the priest were standing there beside me. The cloud of birds fell to the ground and broke into a thousand pieces of black paper. Suddenly a tall man—taller than any I had ever seen— stood between us and Detra Ann. I could not see his face; a gauzy black fog covered his entire body, and only his pale white hands were clearly visible. He did not speak, but his head rose as he observed us.

"Help us." I said to the priest.

Father Portier said in a sad voice, "There is nothing I can do. He is here to collect a life. If I had one to give, I would gladly give it for your friend. But alas I do not. I am sorry, my dear."

"But it wasn't her fault. She never asked for this! We didn't do anything wrong! For pity's sake, Father. Please do something."

He nodded sadly and said again, "I am sorry, my dear."

I heard Detra Ann crying behind the tall figure, and I walked ahead a few more steps. "You can't have her! It's not her time!" Death did not respond, but neither did he move. Then his answer came. He beckoned me toward him, and I knew what he wanted. He wanted me. He would take me in exchange for Detra Ann. *A life for a life….* I heard the words ringing in my head.

Death waited for my answer. *What about the baby?* Fear washed over me, and tears rolled down my cheeks. Then there was Lenore. "I've got this," she whispered. She stood, hopping up and down in her hand-me-down Reeboks as if she were gearing up for a prize fight. It didn't take a rocket scientist to see she was about to do something stupid.

"Wait! What are you doing?"

"Thinking about someone else for a change!" She grabbed my hands and hugged me. "I knew this was how it was supposed to be. I knew it when I met Detra Ann. She's not the only shade here. I'm one too—I've been one ever since Aleezabeth died. It should have been me that day."

"I don't understand," I confessed. The figure in front of us growled, but Lenore didn't appear moved by it.

"I cheated Death once too. I've been running all these years, but it's time to stop. This is what's right. This is what Aleezabeth wants." She hugged me again and suddenly released me. Then she ran toward the growling figure, screaming, "Aleezabeth!"

I yelled at the top of my lungs, "Lenore! No! Come back!" I watched in horror as she sprang into the air and fearlessly hurled herself toward Death. Then the massive shape vanished, taking Lenore with it. Everything changed. All the coldness, the fear and the dread vanished—even the interior of the church was different. I could smell the freshly painted white walls; the sooty sconces had been replaced with modern-day pin lights that shone from the ceiling. I stood rocking on my heels in shock at the transformation.

I tried to process what had just happened. Lenore had given her life for Detra Ann. My friend lay crumpled on the floor, and I ran to her side.

"Detra Ann! Wake up. Please wake up!" I patted her face desperately. I had to know she was okay.

Her eyes fluttered open, and she looked up at me. "Is it gone?"

"Yes. It's over." We held one another, both of us crying, and then she asked me. "Where is Lenore? I saw her—you came for me. Is Henri okay? Ashland?"

"The guys are fine. Lenore is…she's gone."

"Oh no…" she cried and held onto me as I helped her up from the marble floor. The priest had disappeared too. Detra Ann and I alone stood in the church together, holding one another until Ashland and Henri came up from the basement and ran down the aisle toward us.

"Carrie Jo? Are you okay, baby? Why are you bleeding?"

I glanced down at my hands. He was right—they were bleeding. "It's okay. I'm okay." He put his arms around me and kissed the top of my head.

Henri held Detra Ann tight, tears streaming down his face. "Lenore, where is she?"

"She's gone, Henri," I said softly. "She wanted to be with Aleezabeth. She said it was right."

Detra Ann held him closer and whispered in his ear. I couldn't hear what she said, but I didn't need to know. They had each other now. He nodded and wiped his eyes. This would be hard for him. Lenore was all the family he had. Except us. We were a family. A strange, wonderful family.

Chapter Sixteen—Carrie Jo

The next few days were strange to say the least. I felt like I was walking in a fog. I closed the office while we worked out the details of Lenore's memorial service, then the four of us took the Happy Go Lucky out into Mobile Bay. The only one who seemed truly happy was Detra Ann, and who could blame her? Our first evening out was quiet. The water was like smooth glass, and the air felt warm and welcoming. We were sailing to Point Clear, where we would stay for a few days. With just a quick phone call, Ashland had managed to book two suites at the Grand Hotel. It was a beautiful place with a breathtaking view of the bay. Naturally, I was fascinated with the history of the place and promised myself that sometime during my stay I would explore the older wings and the grounds.

After dinner on the boat, Ashland and I spent an hour looking out over the bay, enjoying the lights and the stars that glittered above it all. We held hands and quietly enjoyed the peaceful view.

"How are you?" he asked softly, his eyes still focused in front of us.

"I'm fine. The baby is too. Everything is okay."

"That's good to hear."

"What about you? How are you doing with all this?"

"I haven't seen anything in forty-eight hours. Any ghosts, I mean. It's like everything went quiet again. It's times like this when I question if I ever saw any of what I thought I saw. But I know I did."

"Don't question it. You did see those things. Just enjoy the quiet for as long as it lasts." I smiled at him and squeezed his hand. Then I asked, "Are you sure you want to stay in Mobile, Ashland? I think the Port City has more than its share of ghosts, don't you?"

"I love Mobile, but I want you to be happy. Do you want to leave?"

I squinted at him in the dim light. "Nope. You're stuck with me, babe. Wherever you are—that's where I want to be. We made a promise, remember?" I slid out of the white leather chair and climbed into his lap.

He kissed me like he meant it. I kissed him back, and I definitely meant it. With a wicked smile, I led him to the shower, stripping off my clothes as I went. I loved this ridiculously large shower stall. It had four shower heads, a smooth stone floor and sultry blue lighting. Just perfect for what I had in mind. I kicked on the wall stereo and turned on the water as Ashland raced to join me. It was a nice way to end the day.

Afterwards, I pulled on a giant t-shirt and climbed into the feather bed and fell asleep almost immediately. For once, I didn't have a worry in the world.

***

I woke up with Hooney's face so close to mine that I could feel her breath on my cheek. She whispered to me, but I was half asleep and had difficulty understanding what she said.

"Your mother wants you to go. Leave this place, Miss Calpurnia. Leave now."

I had given up trying to convince the old woman that I was not my sister. In a perverse sort of way, the misidentification made me feel closer to Calpurnia.

"Why? Why should I go?" I pressed her, but Hooney's tight grimace let me know that I would get nothing else out of her. She had passed on the message and believed it should be enough. "Where is my mother? Why does she not tell me this herself, Hooney?"

"You know good and well why." I heard a noise from the hallway…someone was here! Karah was not in the room with me, and I could see that her rose pink dress was no longer hanging in the armoire. She must have dressed in one of the other rooms because she never dressed quietly. That meant Isla would be here any moment—if she had not yet arrived.

"Tell me, is Karah's mother here? I have to get dressed."

"She is, Miss. But if I were you, I would run the other way. She's the devil, that one." With that, the old woman left me without another word or glance. I flopped on the bed wondering what to do. If Hooney was truly relaying messages from my mother, was I wise to ignore them? I snorted at myself. When did I begin believing in ghosts? Gooseflesh ran up and down my arms. Then I remembered. Probably when I saw the man in the Moonlight Garden…the one whose hair did not move in the breeze!

I dressed quickly and managed to arrange my hair in a decent fashion with the few pins that I found remaining in the bowl on the vanity table. Sliding on my purple heels, I dabbed perfume on my neck and headed toward the stairs when I heard Karah's voice. The sound was coming from the guest room, so I politely tapped on the door and waited. Nobody came, but I could still hear muffled voices. With a frown, I opened the door slowly and hoped it wouldn't give me away. Of course, it groaned as I pushed it open, and I cringed. "Karah, I am sorry to interrupt, but I could not wait to meet your..."

I left off speaking, surprised to see that no one was in the room. There were trunks and packages everywhere; obviously Cousin Isla intended to stay in this room. I heard the voices again and followed the source. I discovered that the sounds were coming from the floor grate. Not wanting to intrude, I turned to walk away, but something in Karah's voice compelled me to listen.

"Please, Mother. You could not be more wrong. She is not your enemy or mine. I like her!"

"You always...take my side for a change...weak, just like your father!" Isla's voice wasn't as clear. It sounded like she was moving about. Where were they? The Blue Room? "Maybe you have already found it. Are you keeping it from me, Karah?"

"Never! I would never do that, Mother. I have searched high and low, and I cannot find it. I swear to you, I do not have it!"

"If that is true, you had better get her out of here before she finds it. Oh, if only you had been a boy. None of this would matter."

I heard Karah's voice, soft and sad, "I am sorry, Mother. I will find it if it takes me..."

"What are you doing there, Miss Page?"

I rose from the floor to find Docie in the doorway, her arms crossed. She wore her usual black dress and severe bun. I stammered, "Well, I thought I heard Karah, but I was mistaken. Nobody is here." I walked towards the doorway, intending to slip out, but Docie would not let me pass.

"You should not be in here without an invitation. This is Miss Beaumont's room, and she is very particular about her things." She suddenly frowned and walked to an open trunk, examining the sumptuous gowns inside. "You have not touched these, have you?"

"No, of course not."

"Good. You will stain her fine gowns. Such lovely fabrics, don't you agree? It would be a crime to damage such an elegant wardrobe."

The voices from the grate had faded; the women had obviously left the room below us. "Very fine. Excuse me."

"Wait, Miss Page."

I froze in the hallway, and Docie purred, "Remember my warning. I hope I make myself clear." I knew that was a threat, and I would be a fool not to heed it. Docie was dangerous, and it sounded as if her mistress had a secret of her own.

Instead of running downstairs to greet Karah's mother, I went back to my room to catch my breath. I knew that Karah had been looking for something, but what? A book, a love letter, a will? The only way I would find out would be to ask her, but I did not want to put my cousin in such a position. Her mother sounded like a hard woman to please. After seeing Isla's gowns, I changed mine, choosing instead a bright yellow dress with plenty of lace and a respectable neckline. I loathed the idea of presenting myself as the "poor cousin" who had nowhere to go. I was a dressmaker, for goodness' sake! I changed shoes and earrings too and then headed towards the stairs for a second time.

There was no one in the ladies' parlor, but I could hear the musical sound of tinkling laughter. The beautiful Isla Beaumont was now holding court on the patio near the Rose Garden. From the half-open door I could see Jackson Keene, Karah and a man I did not recognize listening to a riveting story told as only an actress could. Isla was the most beautiful woman I had ever seen, with dainty facial features and hair like an angel's, blond and perfectly curled. Even though she was Karah's mother, she barely looked old enough to have had a child. Isla paused her monologue and tilted her head toward me.

"Come now. Don't be shy." I immediately felt embarrassed to have been spotted dawdling behind the door like an awkward child. She rose to her feet and neatly arranged her ethereal blue dress before making a beeline for me. "You must be Delilah. I am Isla Beaumont." I felt ill at ease, perhaps because all her attention seemed to rest upon me now. It was as intense as her storytelling had been.

I blushed and said, "I am Delilah Page. And you are Karah's mother. It is very nice to meet you at last." The older woman flinched at my words even though I could not fathom why. Had I offended her already?

"You do have the look of your sister. I am sure you hear that all the time."

"Only since I have been here, but I never tire of hearing it. You knew her?"

"We spoke a few times."

"A few times? Surely you jest, dear Miss Beaumont. You were Miss Cottonwood's constant companion for some time. I've often wondered how she managed to escape Seven Sisters without your knowing anything about it." The man who spoke to her had a round belly, a balding head and an obvious love for sweets. Even

now his fingers could not resist plucking sugared grapes from the silver platter on a nearby table.

"Why yes, Mr. Ball, we did spend some time together. But Calpurnia was very shy and not one for social gatherings, and as you know, I spent much of my time out and about getting to know our neighbors. Ah, but that was before the dreadful old war. Tell me, Delilah, do you suffer the same maladies as your sister?"

I blinked at her, unsure how I should respond. "What do you mean? What maladies?"

She giggled and smiled at the audience watching us. "Am I speaking out of turn? Please forgive me, Karah. You know what I speak of, Mr. Ball. But I promised Karah I would not embarrass you, dear girl. Come join us, Delilah. What a lovely name! Have you ever considered becoming an actress? You have the name for it, you know. I wonder why your mother bestowed such a name on you. Not a very proper name, is it, and Christine Cottonwood was nothing but proper. Or so we all thought." She giggled again as if she knew some great joke and I was the butt of it. Sadness welled up in me. This woman did not like me, and I had so wanted her to. The gathering appeared shocked and embarrassed by her description of my mother, but nobody said a thing against her. My first instinct was usually wrong, as Maundy often reminded me. So I kept my mouth shut and sat quietly listening to Isla's news about the London stage and how wonderfully she had played Claudia DuMont in some play called "The Delight of New York." Everyone nodded and asked the appropriate questions, but I could not help but notice she did not look in my direction again or shower her smiles upon me. Those she reserved for the men and occasionally for her faithful servant, Docie, who was never more than a few feet away from her mistress. Karah appeared to be as miserable as I was, but there was something else there too. I could not understand it. I watched the silent interactions carefully, just as I had been trained to in the dress shop. It was obvious that Docie worshipped Isla and waited on her as if she were the Queen of England. Karah seemed a mere afterthought to her mother. Isla had a way of selfishly stealing all the air out of a room.

Jackson Keene received more than his share of Isla's attentions, and I wasn't the only one who noticed. Karah's pretty face was awash with red color, obviously flushed with embarrassment at her mother's forwardness. Once Isla even touched Jackson's leg as she spoke. Although she acted like it was an accident, I believed no such thing. As quickly as I could politely arrange it, I excused myself; I was eager to remove myself from her presence. But where would I go?

As I walked through the patio door into the ladies' parlor and then down the downstairs hallway, Docie followed me, watching every step I took.

"May I help you, Docie?"

"No, miss." She did not move but stood in the hallway like a sentinel, her hands clasped in front of her. I wanted to go upstairs and hide, but then thankfully Jackson stepped into the hallway.

"Miss Page, may I speak to you for a moment?"

"Yes, of course. Why don't you take a walk with me, Mr. Keene? It's a lovely night, and it's much too stuffy in here."

"Indeed it is."

As soon as our feet hit the path of the Moonlight Garden, I felt the burden lift. "What do you think of Isla Beaumont, Jackson?"

He mulled over his answer and then said, "How can the daughter be so different from the mother? Karah is the picture of virtuousness, but her mother has no such restraint." That wasn't exactly the answer I had expected. I had no idea that Jackson thought so highly of Miss Cottonwood. He looked about him; when he was finally convinced that no one was listening he said, "I have had a difficult time of proving your cousin's parentage." We strolled down the brick path together, circled the fountain and walked into the garden maze. "Everyone in the county says that her mother was never a respectable young woman. Isla herself was born out of wedlock, and now her daughter shares her status." He glanced over and added quickly, "I mean no insult. I am merely repeating what others have said."

"That is gossip, Jackson, and I am surprised to hear you repeat it."

"No, it is fact. As Miss Cottonwood's attorney, I have a professional duty to investigate these matters. Supposedly, Miss Beaumont took up with a riverboat captain, a David Garrett, but he was murdered a few years ago. By all accounts he was a man of few restraints. I should not like to shock you, but I have it on good authority that this Captain Garrett once had designs on your sister, until he met Miss Beaumont. After that, he cared for no other woman. I am almost convinced that he is Karah's true father, but what can I do?"

"I can hardly believe what I am hearing. No wonder Isla does not like me—I take it she was no friend of my sister's, then?"

"Not in the truest sense of the word, no. And to make matters more complicated, she had an affair with Jeremiah Cottonwood, while he was married to your mother."

"I see," I said as I pondered what he had told me.

"However, I have good news to share. I have had an offer from Claudette Page. Would you like to hear it? Perhaps I should wait until tomorrow to tell you the details?"

"No, please I want to hear her offer now. I need something else to think about." I sat on a nearby bench and waited.

"Very well. Your aunt came to my office yesterday and says she will agree to acknowledge you in name and will not contest any deed you possess if you agree to leave Mobile. She says she will give you everything that her brother wanted you to have but insists that you must leave and remain away from the city until her death."

I shot up from the bench. "How dare she ask me to leave? How can I leave Karah and Seven Sisters?"

"My dear, Karah could always come visit you wherever you reside. Think about what this would mean. You would never have to work again—no more late nights at Miss Weaver's shop. You could travel and see the world. With this act, Miss Page has sealed your future. You are a very wealthy woman now, Delilah. The world is your oyster!"

Exasperated, I stormed off, walking deeper into the garden.

"Delilah! Wait!"

"You don't understand, Jackson! It was never about the money."

"Please, just think about this."

"No! And don't follow me!" I turned to the left, then to the right and then to the left again, slapping branches out of my way as I went. After all this time, Jackson still didn't understand. Yes, I would have money and possessions, but I would still be denied the thing I wanted most—a family! I wanted to belong

*somewhere...to someone. Claudette Page was willing to sacrifice
her fortune to see that I never had that.*

*I was so angry that I barely noticed the dark-haired man
watching me from the other side of the clearing. Yes! There he
was—near the Atlas fountain. It was the same man who had
followed me the other night. I froze on the spot. He smiled, and
my stomach twisted. I turned to walk away and nearly walked
into Isla Beaumont.*

*Her eyes were fierce—she reminded me of a wild animal. One
that was trapped inside the body of an innocent sheep and
desperately wanted to be released. "Oh, sorry. I didn't hear you,"
I said. "I think we should go, Miss Beaumont. There is an
intruder in our garden."*

*She stared at me and then turned her attention to the man
standing at the Atlas fountain. She could see him too! The wind
picked up, sending her ethereal blue dress fluttering. I just watched
as she took down her hair and let her blond tresses blow freely
behind her. I looked from her to him and felt my unease growing.*

*She took my hand and tugged on it, dragging me after her. She
was walking toward the man and taking me with her! He hadn't
moved, but he had an evil smile plastered on his pale face. "Let go
of me!" I yelled at her, wrenching my hand free from her deathly
grip. She did not seem to notice. She continued toward him as the
wind continued to blow.*

*I ran! I ran as fast as I could all the way back to the entrance of
the maze. I ran so fast that I collided with Jackson Keene. "There
you are," he said, steadying me. "Have you changed your mind?
Delilah, what is it?"*

"Didn't you see Isla? She was just here with that man. The evil-looking one with the dark hair. He...she...they are just in there."

"Nobody came out here. Just you and me. I wish you would reconsider Claudette's offer. I do believe she is being sincere."

"Very well. Make the arrangements. I am ready to leave Mobile." With one more glance over my shoulder, I practically ran back into the house. I could hardly believe it...when I passed the ladies' parlor, Isla was still there, regaling her guests, except for Jackson and me, about her experiences on the stage. How could I have seen her just now in the garden with that evil man? With that ghost? As if she knew what I was thinking, she stopped talking and smiled at me innocently.

Yes, I was ready to go. I would go to my room and pack, and then leave first thing in the morning. I heard Jackson's carriage leave almost immediately, but I went upstairs and asked Hooney to help me pack. I went to my mother's room and plundered her hope chest and treasures. If I was going to leave, I would take something of hers with me. Karah had told me repeatedly to take whatever I liked. She had no need of it. In fact, she hinted that when her mother left Seven Sisters, she wished to go with her. Then no one would live here, except a few forgotten former slaves.

I found a few books, ribbons and sewing pieces that I decided to take with me. Walking back to my room, Hooney surprised me by bringing supper to me. I ate it, hungry now that I did not have to entertain Isla any longer. "Please ask Stokes to come get my things, Hooney. I am going to stay in town tonight."

"It's too late, Miss Calpurnia. Stokes isn't here now. He had to go somewhere for that lady. I suspect he won't be home until late."

I tried to keep the tremor out of my voice as I replied, "Well, I can send for these things tomorrow. I'll just take one bag with me." My hands shook as I sorted through everything. Just as I was ready to leave, Isla walked into my room. Hooney scurried out, making the sign of the cross as she went.

"What's this, cousin? Are you leaving when I just got here? I was hoping we would have some fun, get to know one another. I have so much to tell you."

"I saw you in the garden, Isla. I saw you with that man." I said, nervously clutching my bag. "I think I will stay in town tonight. Stokes can bring my things tomorrow."

"Hmm…you act like you are the lady of the house here, Delilah. You don't command my servants. In regards to what you think you saw, I must confess I am at a loss as to what you mean." Then in a sad, sweet voice she added, "You know, those are just the maladies I was referring to when I spoke about your sister. She had…such an imagination. It must be a trait the two of you inherited from your father. A Beaumont would never go about saying such things."

"How dare you…"

"How dare I what? Tell you the truth?" She sat on the bed and ran her hands across the leather suitcase. As quick as lightning she opened it and began rummaging through my things. She plucked out the things that belonged to my mother. "This is thievery," she said indignantly as she rose from the bed. "Are you stealing from me, cousin?"

"These are my mother's things. You can't stop me from taking them."

"Everything in this house belongs to me." Her voice sounded sharp and angry. *"You put those things back, or I will call the sheriff and he can settle this."*

"You would call the sheriff to report a sewing kit and a few keepsakes? I can't believe it!"

"You should believe it."

Just then Karah poked her head in the room. *"Are you leaving, Delilah?"*

"Yes, I am afraid I must. Thank you for your hospitality, Karah."

She went to hug me, but Isla prevented it. *"You are not leaving with these things. You empty those cases now! I do not make empty threats—just ask my daughter."*

"Mother, I told her she could have a few of her mother's treasures. Surely that is permissible."

Isla slapped her across the face. *"Get out!"* Karah scurried out of the room sobbing.

I grabbed Isla's arms and shook her. *"How dare you hit her? You evil woman! Don't ever touch her again!"*

To my utter surprise, she smiled and then kissed me. In revulsion I pushed her away and ran out the door after Karah. *"Karah! Where are you?"* She was not in her room, and Hooney was nowhere to be found. The balcony door overlooking the Moonlight Garden was open, and I walked toward it. *"Karah!"* I did not see her and turned to walk back inside when Isla stepped in my path.

"Move out of my way!" I said angrily, but she only laughed. Then her beautiful face hardened. She shoved me toward the balcony, and I fell to the floor. "What do you think you're doing, Isla?"

"I am doing what I should have done a long time ago. I should have done it when you were too stupid to know who you were, but it is no matter. You are worm food now, I suppose." She giggled as she brandished an evil-looking knife.

"Oh God, what are you doing?" I lay sprawled on the floor, my mind racing. I looked about me, hoping to find something to defend myself with. But there was nothing, only a chair and a table. "Why are you doing this, Isla? I am your blood."

"Now, now, don't be difficult. Be still, cousin. I don't want to get your blood all over my new dress." The knife arced toward me as I rolled and scrambled to my feet. I was standing now, but she still blocked the only exit. "Very well. If you prefer to jump, I won't stop you. Go ahead." She pointed her knife to the balcony's edge.

"No!" I shouted. "Karah!"

"Leave my daughter out of this unless you want to get her killed too. Now be a good girl and do as I tell you. Keep moving—this will all be over soon." I heard a noise below and saw Karah looking up at me. Isla sliced my arm with the blade, and I screamed.

"No! Go away!" I kicked the chair at her as I cried and moved out of her reach. Blood poured down my arm as she herded me to the edge of the balcony just as she'd promised. "What do you want? Why are you doing this?"

"Since the first day I arrived here, I knew this was mine. My adulteress sister didn't deserve this place—neither did her fool of a *daughter. Calpurnia was so stupid—it was mind-numbingly easy to make her believe that David loved her, but he never did. He only ever loved me!" She shouted and waved her knife. "Now there is just one untidy loose end left. You. The forgotten bastard. I told Claudette that you wouldn't be so easily dissuaded, but she was too proper to agree to my solution. But here we are, just the two of us. I sent Stokes away, and Hooney is so old and blind, she'd never hear you even if you cried day and night."*

My back was against the railing now. There was nowhere else for me to go. Only down, down, down to my death. I looked down again but only for a second in case she sliced me again. "Help me! Somebody!" I screamed into the fading light. Nobody answered. I turned to see Isla waving her blade again, and this time she tore through my dress and cut my abdomen. I cried out in pain.

"Mother! Stop it!" Karah reached for an old wooden cane that stood in a bucket near the doorway. She raised it high and swung at her mother.

Isla crumpled to the ground and squealed angrily. "Stupid girl!" She clutched her arm and reached for her knife.

"Stop, Mother! You are out of your mind!"

"Such a coward! How could I have raised such a coward? I never wanted you, did you know that? All I ever wanted was my captain—and my home. That's all I ever wanted. Now you want to throw it all away like it meant nothing. Like what I did meant nothing. You stupid coward!" She ran toward us with her knife raised, but Karah struck her again. She fell again, but I knew it wouldn't stop her—she was truly mad.

"Run, Delilah!" My arm was slick with my own blood and I felt cold, but I tried to keep up with her. Then Docie appeared at the

top of the stairs, her hands in her pockets and a murderous look on her face.

"Stop them, Docie!" Isla yelled as she tried to stand after Karah's latest attack.

"You heard the mistress. Where do you think you're going?" Karah's face turned white, and I could see fear arresting her reasoning. It was my turn to do something. I snatched the cane and swung it toward Docie, hitting her square in the stomach. Without a sound she fell backwards down the stairs and landed at the bottom, her head turned at an awkward angle. Karah pulled me out of the way as Isla ran toward her, leaving her knife behind.

"No! Docie!"

"Run, Karah! Come with me!" We scrambled down the stairs and out the back of the house. A half hour later, my cousin and I appeared at Jackson's door, and the last thing I remembered was Jackson lifting me out of the carriage in his strong arms. How I wanted to stay in his arms forever...

***

The first thing I did when I woke up was examine my arms. I had felt every painful slice Delilah had endured, and I was happy to see that those wounds had not followed me into my own life. I tried to still my breathing, and the baby fluttered about as if he too had seen and experienced the drama. I hoped I was wrong about that. I hoped Lenore was wrong.

Shh...sweet little one. It's all right now. We're safe.

As always, I reviewed what I dreamed, remembering details I thought would be important later. That surely hadn't been the end of Delilah—I knew she had become a celebrated actress. But what about her and Jackson? Did they have a happily ever after? It would be nice to know that someone in Ashland's family did. Ashland stirred beside me and put his arm around me. I lay back down and snuggled up next to him.

"Still dreaming, Carrie Jo?"

"Yes, still dreaming."

"How about this once you just dream about us?"

"I like that idea. Now how do I do it?" I sighed, feeling tired but suddenly very peaceful.

With a devilish smile and a twinkle in his blue eyes, he whispered, "Let me help you with that."

With a smile of my own I agreed.

Read more from M.L. Bullock

The Seven Sisters Series

Seven Sisters
Moonlight Falls on Seven Sisters
Shadows Stir at Seven Sisters
The Stars that Fell
The Stars We Walked Upon
The Sun Rises Over Seven Sisters (forthcoming)

The Desert Queen Series

The Tale of Nefret
The Falcon Rises
The Kingdom of Nefertiti
The Song of the Bee-Eater (forthcoming)

The Sugar Hill Series (forthcoming)

Wife of the Left Hand
The Ramparts
Blood By Candlelight

The Sirens Gate Series (forthcoming)

The Mermaid's Gift
The Blood Feud
The Wrath of Minerva
The Lorelei Curse
The Fortunate Star

The Southern Gothic Series

Being with Beau

To receive updates on her latest releases,
visit her website at MLBullock.com
and subscribe to her mailing list.

CPSIA information can be obtained
at www.ICGtesting.com
Printed in the USA
LVHW04s2044190718
584344LV00011B/1077/P